# A NORTHWEST SAGA

## THE LIFE AND TIMES OF PETE ECKLAND

*By*

**Stan Young**

# Table of Contents

# *Prologue*

The vast Pacific Northwest, encompassing Oregon, Washington, British Columbia, and Alaska, is one of Earth's choicest regions. It is blessed with thousands of miles of spectacular ocean shorelines, majestic mountain ranges, mighty rivers, boundless forests, and all the fish and wildlife one could wish. Once home to Indians and Eskimos, there's now a modern-day and bustling society with a versatile and thriving economy.

This saga portrays the life and times of one northwesterner, Pete Eckland, over a span of the past forty years, and chronicles his many diverse activities and endeavors.

Pete was born, raised, and resides in Bellingham, Washington. With a zest for living and energized by all the vast region has to offer, he fishes, hunts, discovers gold, manages a congressman's office, teaches, writes books, espouses *green conservatism*, and is president of a university. He's resolute in striving to save native fish runs, protect the environment, solve thorny political problems, and confront bigotry. He also is happily married to Leah and father of twin sons, Einar and Bruce.

His is an altogether busy, productive, and rewarding existence, but not without challenges, the kind one might expect in such a varied and exciting region.

Northwest residents, particularly those of long standing, and others as well, are sure to relate to the sequence and nature of his fulfilling life, and find his experiences, beliefs, and deeds familiar and meaningful. Some may even find a few provocative.

**************

The story-line is fiction, as are the characters. *Granddad's* experiences in Yellowstone's Thorofare and Bechler are based on real events and people during the time the author was a fire-guard there the summers of 1946 and 1947.

# BOOK ONE. DISCOVERY

## Chapter One

My name's Pete Eckland and I am a native of Bellingham, Washington, having been born and raised there. After serving three years in the Army, including eighteen months in Vietnam, I've only recently returned. It's mid-September and I'm soon to begin my freshman year at the college in Bellingham. Right now I'm standing alongside one of the North Cascade's more enticing steelhead rivers as it wends its way west before joining Puget Sound near Bellingham.

Fly fishing for summer steelhead was my favorite sport prior to entering the Army, and this river was one I usually counted on for top action. I'd hoped to pick up where I left off three years ago, but after several long days, only one steelhead's come to my fly. It's probably because the river is unusually low and clear and the fish spooky.

With only a few days remaining before beginning college, I'm pondering what to do next. Shall I stay put and hope it rains and the fish start biting, move to another river, or return to Bellingham?

As I glance about, another possibility comes to mind. A side canyon next to where my car's parked supports a small stream and appears to extend south quite a distance. Why not hike up and see what it has to offer? On earlier pre-Army trips, I'd thought of doing this, but never got around to it because the main river was such good fishing. But, what's to lose?

Stuffing my backpack with camping gear and several days of food, grabbing my fishing rod and shotgun, and I'm off. One hope is that the little stream has fish, maybe even steelhead.

After several miles, the canyon, steep and narrow at first, begins leveling out and opening up. At about seven miles, the trail leads out across an expansive meadow with the stream down the middle. In the center, near the stream, is an old homestead, obviously long abandoned. At the meadow's lower end, behind an old earthen dam, is a pond.

Captivated with all that's before me, I decide to spend the night. So, crossing to a grassy area between the old homestead and stream, I select a spot to camp. The only signs of use are two fire-rings, probably where deer or elk hunters once camped. The long hike in and lack of a road would discourage most users.

After pitching my tent and gathering campfire

wood, I take my rod and walk to where the stream leaves the forest and begins meandering across the meadow. Fringed with scattered low bushes and featuring a series of intriguing pools and pockets, it appears made to order for trout. Working downstream and flicking my fly to likely spots, almost every cast brings a strike. All are rainbows, to about twelve inches. One's kept for breakfast.

Nearing the pond, I note that it's about fifty yards long, thirty yards wide near the old dam, and maybe as much as eight feet deep down the middle. The water flows steadily before dropping through a breach in the dam. Steelhead appear a definite possibility.

Approaching cautiously and keeping a low profile, I cast where the stream enters the pond. Nothing. After covering the pond's full length, still nothing. Have I spooked them, or aren't there any?

Returning to camp, I plan trying the pond again in the morning, but evening's at hand and dinner beckons. After eating, I go to the old homestead for an idea of what's there. Looking about, I see a house and several side structures. The house, except for a rickety front door and some missing and broken windows, appears intact and quite sturdy. A glance inside reveals primitive furniture, an old iron stove, and an assortment of kitchen ware. Inevitably, pack rats have been busy.

Off to the side, there's a small tool shed. Also, the remains of a barn, root cellar, and out-house. But it's late and I'm ready for sleep, so I return to camp.

Next morning, first light, I'm back at the pond hoping to spot steelhead surfacing, something they often do then. Seeing none, I again begin casting where the stream enters. The second cast answers whether any are present. There's a swirl, pull, and a hefty fish is on. After five minutes of exciting back and forth dashes and leaps, a bright steelhead of about five pounds is reeled in and released. If there's one, there may be others, but the pond needs resting. So I return to camp for a breakfast of trout rolled in flour and fried with bacon, a bowl of oatmeal, and a cup of tea.

After eating, the pond rewards me with another about the same size. Then, with a lunch and my rod and shotgun, I'm away to see what the stream and canyon farther up are like, and whether there are mushrooms and grouse.

The trail, including traces of an old road probably dating back to early logging, continues up the canyon. After several miles and while glimpsing the stream in a few places but finding it too difficult to fish because of the dense brush, I turn back. At one point, angling up through a patch of second growth Douglas fir, I spot the distinctive yellow of a patch of chanterelle mushrooms. Only a few, but enough.

Needing a grouse, as I approach the meadow, one flushes from a tree and is downed.

Its mid afternoon and time for a closer look at the old homestead. Envisioning what surviving must have been like in such an isolated location with no neighbors, I figure summers wouldn't have been too difficult, but winters, brutal. Meat wouldn't have been a problem with all the fish and game, but what about the other necessities? More needs to be learned.

With evening at hand, I roast a grouse over campfire coals, fry up a mix of mushrooms and onions, and prepare a bowl of freshly gathered watercress and dandelion greens, garnished with olive oil and vinegar. Tasty and filling.

A little later, bedded in my tent, I reflect on what's proving to be a rewarding trek. My only regret is not having attempted it before now. I also think back over some of the seminal events that shaped my life.

Only child of an ardent angling father, from when I first was able to cast a fly, he never missed a chance having me along as he traveled from river to river throughout the Northwest. Sadly, both he and my mother were killed when their car was struck by a logging truck. This, when I was eighteen. Grief-stricken and alone and not knowing what to do or where to turn, I enlisted in the Army. The military provided the succor I needed at the time.

Arising next morning, I enjoy another meal of trout, oatmeal, and tea. While eating, it's impossible not being entranced by all I see, hear, and feel. Early morning's when the natural world's at its freshest and magical best. Across the meadow, several deer browse along the forest edge. A family of mink scurries along the stream. What I'm experiencing is much as the old homesteaders must have known. Wolves and grizzlies no longer roam the area, but otherwise it's essentially as it was then.

When it begins raining and appears likely to continue and increase, I decide to pack up and leave. Two hours later, I'm back where my car's parked.

I now know the little stream has what's needed to nurture a particular strain of summer steelhead, including the required deep pools where they're able to overwinter safely prior to spawning next spring. Drawn by natal instincts up the main river, they await rains that provide enough flow for them to reenter and ascend where they had been reared. Thanks to an inborn small size and rugged tenacity, they're able to survive the little stream's rigors.

The past two days have been exciting. The beautiful meadow and intriguing old homestead, plus the fish, grouse, and mushrooms, are all I could have wished.

What I couldn't foresee is the pivotal role the side canyon and old homestead are destined to play in the coming years.

# Chapter Two

Following my freshman year at College where I'm majoring in Ecology, and two months crewing on a fishing boat out of Kodiak, Alaska, it's mid-September and I'm eager to revisit to the old homestead. I may spend as much as a week before returning for my sophomore year.

Before going, I drop by the local Forest Service office in hopes of learning something about the place. Standing alongside a large wall map with Jerry Green, a Forest Service clerk, I point to the meadow and ask, "Last year I hiked to this location and found an old homestead. Would your records have any information about the place, including its former occupants?"

He consults a file and says, "Our records show that the old homestead and all the surrounding lands are part of the national forest and have been ever since the Forest Service began administering the area, many years ago. But they don't include anything about who once lived there."

He then suggests, "Jed Smith may know. He's an old timer who once homesteaded near there. Almost ninety, he lives here in town. Check also with the county clerk, she may know something." As I leave, he hands me a national forest map, and tells me where to find Jed Smith.

Hoping Mr. Smith's able to shed some light, I drop by his house and find him relaxing in the back yard. After introductions, I spread the national forest map out between us and, pointing to the location of the old homestead, explain, "I just came from the local Forest Service office where I was told that you once homesteaded in the same general area and might know something about the place and its former occupants. I hiked there a year ago, became interested, and plan to return."

"Yes, I still recall something of the old homestead. A man and his wife, after moving west from Tennessee, were searching for a place to settle down, visited that location, liked what they found, and decided to stay. I believe it was about 1910. The region had almost no settlers then.

"I came several years later and homesteaded the next canyon over, about ten miles away. They already were well established. No doubt they survived as I did by living off the land. I rode my horse over a few times on visits and was impressed with how well built the house and other structures appeared, and by the small lake he'd created by damming the stream. Got to know them a little, but it was so long ago, I no longer remember their names." And, with a wink, "I suspect they may have brewed a little moonshine.

"The last time I got there, about 1920, the place was deserted. I tried finding what happened, but never learned anything. Supposed they returned to Tennessee where getting by probably was easier."

All this is helpful and makes me even more curious about the place.

Upon reaching the old homestead, I find that the meadow area is just about as it was the year before, except the grass is lusher and the stream has more water. Nothing indicates anyone's been here since.

While doing the usual things, I've decided this time to concentrate mainly on the one thing that intrigues me most, the old homestead and what it may reveal about its former occupants. Are there farm implements that have survived? Is there evidence of livestock, since either a horse or ox would have been needed in constructing the dam? And what about a still for making moonshine? Many questions in need of answers.

But first I set up camp and then go to the stream to see what it has to offer.

With more water, steelhead may have moved

above the pond, so I walk to where the stream enters the meadow and begin slowly casting my way down.  Still lots of trout,  but no steelhead.

Again, anticipating a *take* where the stream enters the pond, I'm not disappointed.  One grabs my fly on almost the first cast and cavorts all over before being brought  in and released.  It's similar in size to those last year.  Good to know there's at least one, but the water needs resting, so I return to camp for dinner.

Having eaten, I'm back again at the old house. Rummaging around inside, I'm curious why most of what they'd accumulated all those years appears still to be here.  They must have taken things when they left, and over the years visitors no doubt had absconded with more, but all the larger items and more remain.

The house rests on a low foundation of mortared river-rocks, with a siding of roughly hewed boards, and a roof of robust cedar shakes.  It's square in shape, fifty feet to a side, and at ground level there are three rooms, including a combination living room and kitchen, and two bedrooms. The roof slants down sharply from a heavy middle beam, beneath which a spacious attic extends over the ceilings of the three rooms.  A ladder leads to the attic from the living room/kitchen area.  The roof is still mostly intact, probably because the cedar shakes are so large and thick and durable.

A tall chimney and indoor fireplace are of the same mortared river-rocks as the foundation. The ancient kitchen stove has a smokestack that projects through the roof. That there are two bedrooms tells me there may have been children. Illumination had to have been by lanterns and candles.

The near-by tool shed, still intact, contains a work bench and wall cabinets. All that remains of the barn and outhouse are collapsed piles of boards. The only other structure is the caved-in root cellar.

Returning to my camp, I relax beside the fire with a book, and then turn in.

First light finds me casting at the pond's upper end. There's a swirl and pull, but no hookup. Continuing the fly across the surface, the fish lunges again and is on. It's similar in size to the others. Along the stream, a twelve inch trout's taken that I have for breakfast.

Intrigued with all that I'm finding in and about the old house, I return for more searching. The collapsed barn first draws my attention because of wanting to confirm what I suspect, that there'd been livestock, likely a horse or ox, possibly a cow and sheep, and maybe chickens. Pulling boards aside, I find an old stall and the rodent eaten remnants of a leather horse halter and reins. A large scoop tells me what had been used to gouge out and drag the earth needed to build the dam. A primitive plow indicates a vegetable garden and, probably, corn for the table. Also, he would have needed corn to make moonshine, but as yet no still.

Next, I go to the tool shed. It's about 15 feet square and holds a few rusting tools and other miscellany. Any implements of value have long since been carted off, but several large horse shoes reveal the size horse used to pull the scoop and plow. Also, there's a pan of the sort used in sifting for gold. Had he panned? Was he successful? I carry the pan back to camp, figuring to give it a try.

The house occupies the rest of my morning. With some repairs, plus removal of the accumulated rodent scat and other litter, it would almost be livable. There are hand-crafted table and chairs and wall cabinets, an assortment of old pots and pans, and various pieces of crockery and eating utensils. The bedrooms still have rudimentary beds, and rodent and moth-eaten remnants of blankets and pillows. There also are a few items of barely discernible clothing, as well as moldy remains of leather shoes.

The attic holds more clothing and household items. I sift through an old trunk and find two tattered books, one a bible and the other a children's book. Spider webs, dust, and rodent nests and scat are everywhere and discourage more than a cursory look.

Finally, I'm beginning to get a feel for the family and an understanding of how they had lived. They undoubtedly were rugged and resourceful individuals; surviving alone in this unforgiving part of Washington would have demanded it. But why, when they left, was so much left behind? That isn't revealed until a later visit.

Pleased with all I've learned this morning, I return to camp, consume a quick lunch, grab my shotgun and a satchel, and head again up the canyon. Before leaving, because fresh bear tracks were found along the stream, I suspend my food from a tree.

Several grouse flush and one falls to my shot. As expected with all the rain, chanterelles are abundant and a supply is soon gathered.

The next morning I take the gold pan to the stream for some trial sifting. The stream crosses the meadow over a bedrock bottom that's strewn with various sized boulders and gravel and sediments washed down during high water. The finer sediments are accumulated in cracks and crevasses along the bottom.

Although never having panned for gold, the idea

had intrigued me and I'd read about it and intended sometime to try it. So I have an idea where to begin and what to do. Using an old shovel and bucket found in the tool shed, I scrounge the stream-bed for sediments. I then gradually parcel them into the pan, while sloshing it back and forth. The lighter sediments wash out and the heavier ones settle. The results are then inspected for *color*.

And color there is. The question is whether it's the real thing, or only *fool's gold*. I remember reading that in sunlight, flakes of fool's gold are indistinguishable from flakes of real gold, but in shade, fool's gold loses its luster while real gold doesn't. In applying the test, it's obvious that most of what I'm finding is fool's gold, but there also are scattered flakes of real gold, plus an occasional tiny gold nugget. This, after several hours' effort. It appears that if I kept at it for an entire day, maybe an ounce could be collected. Gold, I recall, is now worth about $300 an ounce.

Possibly, the homesteaders had panned enough to cover at least a portion of their expenses. They may even have rigged up a sluice box which would have multiplied the amount of sediments they could sift. With that in mind, I return to the tool shed, and then the barn. Beneath more boards, the crushed remnants of what had to have been a sluice box are found.

That the stream has gold and that the homesteaders actually used a sluice box, starts my juices flowing and I decide to learn more about the construction and use of sluice boxes and to bring one next visit.

Out beyond the barn the vestiges of the old root cellar call for a closer look. There's a shattered door and a deep aperture beneath sod-covered supporting beams. Peering down I glimpse collapsed shelves and a few mostly smashed containers that had once been used to hold whatever it was the homesteaders harvested.

Beyond the root cellar, almost hidden by weeds, two foot-square side-by-side flat stones catch my attention. With a little brushing, barely legible carved-in names and dates are revealed. One reads Emma Hicks, 1883-1918, and the other Richard Hicks, 1912-1918. No doubt, mother and son. Possible casualties of the deadly 1918 flu epidemic. Sad, but now I know the homesteaders last name.

Death of wife and son may have been what prompted the husband to abandon the place. In deciding to go, he may not have seen much point in trying to cart off many belongings, and just left. Best simply to leave and start over somewhere else, possibly returning to Tennessee, as Jed Smith had surmised. Perhaps he'd collected enough gold to relocate and get set up in a farm or some kind of business.

All I learned from examining the old house and other structures, in finding the two tombstones and name Hicks, and then discovering the stream actually has gold, have made this visit especially worthwhile.

Already, I'm eagerly anticipating my return next September when some serious gold sluicing is planned. But, another year of college and more Kodiak crewing lie between now and then.

# Chapter Three

The previous autumn I had telephoned Jerry Green, the Forest Service clerk, and told him about finding the two gravestones and the inscribed names and dates. He said he'd do some checking and let me know if he found anything.

About mid-August, soon after I return from Alaska, Jerry telephones. I assume he's going to say something about the Hicks family. Instead, "In July we discovered a large marijuana growing operation near the old homestead, and right now a crew's busy tearing it out. Aerial reconnaissance spotted it because the plants were almost mature and their greenery made them stand out."

"When will it be safe for me to return? I'd hoped to go in September."

"Check back in a week or two and I'll let you know the status of our efforts and when it should be safe. As well as removing the plants, the crew is also dismantling the system used in irrigating the plantings. They soon should be finished. Oh, and another thing, I wasn't able to find any more about the Hicks family you told me about."

So, after checking back early in September and

learning they'd completed the cleanup, I begin hiking up, curious what I'll find. There's now a locked gate, and the trail, once a primitive road, has been improved all the way to the meadow and obviously has recently been in use.

Upon reaching the meadow, abundant signs of the marijuana operation and the effects of its eradication are visible. The growers had planted the marijuana along the forest fringe at the meadow's upper edge, hoping the adjacent trees would screen the plants. Three long rows have been chopped off near ground level.

Jerry said some five thousand plants with a street value of as much as $5 million had been removed. Also, several hundred yards of irrigation piping. The growers made off before they could be apprehended, but a truck load of their gear and provisions left behind had been carted away by the Forest Service.

He advised, "Don't be surprised if you have visitors who appear interested in all that's happened."

The almost pristine conditions I found during my previous two visits no longer exist, both along the meadow's upper edge where the marijuana and piping had been, and in the vicinity of the old house. The grounds around the house are trampled and the house itself has been partially cleaned out and used, including the old fireplace and kitchen stove. They'd even made use of the pit where the outhouse had stood.

Marijuana plants require four or five months to mature, so the operation had been initiated early that spring. The winter, being a mild one with low snowfall, enabled early access.

Rather than camp as before between the stream and house where it's so trampled, I relocate across the stream beneath one of the small trees. In short order a tent is pitched, fire-ring laid, wood gathered, and fly rod assembled. As with the year before, the steam has a healthy flow.

I anticipate that the planters may have fished, and soon learn that's so. Far fewer come to my fly, while enough to meet my needs. The run of summer steelhead wouldn't yet have reached the pool when the planters were present, but some should be there by now.

Evening's at hand and the sun has set behind the mountains and is off the water, a good time to be fishing. I begin at the pool's upper end and within a few casts a steelhead grabs my fly. It's a silvery four pounds and full of fight. I return to camp for dinner.

The next morning finds me assembling a gold sluice from makings I've packed in. That winter I'd bought a kit and learned how to use it. Using a sluice, it's possible in one hour to process as much sediment as it would take a full day using a pan.

While standing at the work bench in the tool shed assembling the sluice, I hear what sounds like a motorcycle. Stepping outside, a cyclist approaches across the meadow.

Pulling up nearby, he waves and in accented English asks, "Nice country, do you live here?"

"No, but I occasionally come to camp and do a little fishing." He isn't aggressive or threatening and after a few more platitudes heads toward where the marijuana had been planted.

Returning to the tool shed and watching through a window, I see him reach the cut rows, dismount, and walk among them. He then remounts and returns the way he'd come. While we were talking, I noticed him glancing at the old house, no doubt checking whether anything remained of their belongings.

I'd heard that marijuana growers often resume their efforts. However, it's too late this year for them to try again, but it could happen next spring, although I doubt it since they must know the Forest Service is on the alert and periodically checking the area. I'm relieved that he's come and gone, and don't expect further visits, at least this year.

Now it's possible to finish assembling the sluice and give it a try.    It's a foot wide and high, five feet long, and easily carried.

Together with the sluice and a bucket and shovel, I move to the stream and begin scrounging cracks and crevasses for sediments and collecting them in the bucket.

Next, I carefully position the sluice in the stream to achieve a flow that    enables    the heavier materials to sink and become trapped in riffles lining the bottom.

Finally, I feed the bucket's contents in at the sluices upper end, gather what's trapped in the riffles, and repeat the process several times, each time with a little faster flow.

When finished, only the heaviest sediments remain, hopefully gold, since it's heaviest of all.    I'd read that gold is 19 times heavier than water.

After spending five hours and sluicing the contents of five buckets, I've collected about a quarter-cup of what I figure are mostly nuggets, possibly weighing eight ounces. But, at $300 an ounce, those several hours have turned out to be surprisingly lucrative.

Over time, as my technique improves, the take should increase. The only thing limiting it will be when there's an end to the gold bearing sediments. But, with over two hundred yards of easily accessible stream across the meadow, plus miles below and above, albeit less accessible, I foresee years of productive sluicing. And, with each period of high water, additional gold-laced sediments wash down.

The discovery calls for prudence. While never aspiring to riches or desiring the fancy baubles some with means indulge themselves, that attitude could inadvertently change.

I also need to be careful in not disclosing the stream's secret to others. Word of what's here could even trigger a mini-gold rush. As to others learning, I figure not to leek the secret, sluice in the presence of others, or flaunt my impending prosperity. No doubt, there'll be questions when the gold's assayed and sold, but they can be deflected.

My new affluence, assuming it holds up, should comfortably carry me through my schooling and get me started in whatever I may choose for a career. I've been relying on the GI Bill, but that won't see me through if I seek an advanced degree. As for my Ecology major, I'm not sure where that's leading.

I remain three more days, dividing my time between sluicing and fishing, hiking, hunting grouse, and gathering mushrooms. Another steelhead is caught.

Deer commonly are spotted mornings and evenings, and one group of five elk use the meadow at night. The pond not only beckons for steelhead, but also for refreshing swims.

For one with my interests and aptitudes, including a craving at times for solitude, the area meets all my needs. That it's surrounded by an extensive and verdant forest and framed on all sides with impressive mountains, only fulfills what I've come to regard as my private Shangri-La.

When I leave, it's with a cup-sized bottle almost full of what appears to be mostly gold nuggets. The sluice is carefully hidden.

Returning to my apartment near the college, the next day I drive south to Everett to get the nuggets assayed. Several assayers are listed in the telephone directory. Going to one, he conducts a *fire* assay. It confirms that, while there are impurities, most of what's in the bottle are nuggets. The mass weighs 24 ounces.

"Gold," he tells me, "currently sells for about $300 an ounce. After discounting for impurities, I estimate that you have about $6,000 worth. If you're interested in selling, I'll buy them for that amount." He asks my name and where I got them.

I say I'm not yet ready to sell, decline revealing

anything about myself or where I obtained them, pay for the assay, and leave.

My plan is to take the nuggets to at least one other assayer. Two days later, I sell them to an assayer in Seattle for $6,500, and deposit the money in my bank account.

For someone accustomed to being on his own and struggling to make ends meet, and facing at least two more years of college, I'm relieved that my financial problems appear to be solved. What a nice turn of events.

# *Chapter Four*

Following spring semester, with plans to spend most my time sluicing, I phone Jerry Green, "Any new marijuana activity?"

"We periodically do fly-over's and so far haven't found any, plus, since it takes four or five months for the plants to grow, the season's too far gone to begin an operation."

Upon arriving, I retrieve the sluice from its hiding place and make a few minor changes to improve its performance. The trout have rebounded and are as abundant as ever, but steelhead have yet to arrive, grouse aren't in season, and it's too early for mushrooms. Consequently, there's little to distract me from sluicing.

Two young backpacking couples happen by one evening and decide to spend the night. They're congenial sorts and join me around my campfire. They too are enrolled at the college and often get off like this, but this is their first time here.

I tell them I regularly come because the area is so inspiring, and to indulge in some fishing, hunting, and mushroom gathering.

The next day, before they head farther up the canyon, I escort them around the old homestead, show them the two grave stones, and tell them some of what I've learned about the place.

They're captivated with everything they see and hear, as well as by the surroundings. Being like-minded individuals, we exchange names and agree that we'll try and get together again at the college.

During the week I gather about three times the amount of nuggets as the previous September.

Owing to the results of my sluicing the year before, I'd already decided to forgo any more *crewing* in Alaska. That freed up time this summer for other pursuits, so several weeks are spent along favorite Washington and Oregon steelhead rivers.

My familiarity with the rivers dated back to when I'd accompanied my father on fishing trips. He'd shown me it was possible to catch even the largest steelhead using small flies and light trout tackle. Nothing quite matched the experience of hooking, fighting, catching, and releasing the mighty fish along the Skagit and Sauk, and such other west-side rivers as the North Stillaguamish, Skykomish, Snoqualmie, and Green. East of the Cascades were the Methow and Wenatchee, and in southern Washington the Klickitat, Wind, Washougal, East Lewis, and Kalama. On the Olympic Peninsula, the Sol Duc, Calama, Bogachiel, Hoh, and Queets excelled.

Oregon's Deschutes, North Umpqua, and Rogue were three others special ones. At one time or another I had fished all of them with my father.

Dad had known Ralph Wahl and sometimes fished with him. Ralph lived along the lower Skagit, and while almost all others were casting spoons or shrimp, he used nothing but flies, regardless of the season. Also a skilled nature photographer and writer, Ralph converted my dad to fly fishing, and my dad never looked back. Thus, I was brought up knowing only flies.

I also get to Vancouver Island for a try at some of the rivers the legendary Roderick Hague-Brown had chronicled in his writings. While most of my time is spent learning where to go and what to do, I manage to catch several.

I'd planned on diving to northern British Columbia to fish some of its famous steelhead rivers for the first time, including the Skeena and its Bulkley, Kispiox, and Morice tributaries, but learned October is when they're best. Since that conflicted with school, I decided to wait until after graduating.

Mid-September I'm back again at the old homestead, this time with archery gear. Bow-hunting for Blacktail bucks is in season and I figure on getting one to supplement my larder the coming winter.

Anticipating success, I pull a light weight two-wheel cart in for carrying the deer out. What with hunting and the others activities, there won't be much time for sluicing, but that's no problem because I'd collected enough nuggets in June to see me through the year.

After setting up camp, I'm at the pond to confirm steelhead having arrived. Some should be there, but it's another dry year. I soon have an answer. Beginning where the stream enters and working a third of the way down, one grabs a waking fly. After the usual spirited fight, a small hen is released.

Before retiring for the night, I scout around the meadow, looking for signs of deer. Lots of fresh tracks along the upper border near the cut-off marijuana plants, so that's where I'll begin in the morning.

Awakening early, I grab a quick breakfast, pack a lunch, and head for the upper border. When no deer are found, I continue up the canyon, walking slowly and peering into the woods on both sides. Mid-morning, at an opening in the woods, I notice a tree with fresh antler rubs. Knowing Blacktails often hang around close to their rubs, I move off a short distance and crouch down behind some low bushes.

A little later, a *flicked* ear near the rub catches my

attention. Glancing over, a small buck's standing broadside. Having already nocked an arrow, I have only to  raise my bow, draw, aim, and release. However, the buck, sensed my presence, jumps away just as the arrow leaves.

I remain a while longer hoping he'll return. When he doesn't, I head back toward camp, hunting along the way. Two does are spotted, but no more bucks.

That evening I hear the bugling of nearby elk. They're in season, but way too much meat. Maybe,  at some future time, but not now.

For one that's so attuned to the out-of-doors, camping in such a remote  location with  the  peace and tranquility it offers and  all the  varied forms  of wildlife close at hand and no signs of civilization other than an occasional airliner seven miles overhead,  I  find  the experience  almost overwhelming.

I dream of fixing up the old house and remaining for weeks, but while tempting, realize it isn't practical considering the realities of my life.  The next best thing is to return whenever possible for a few days of the kind of relaxation and renewal the area provides, as well as to augment my bank account and venison larder.

Rain threatens the next morning.  Rather than hunting, I decide to spend at least part of the day sluicing along a new section of stream. After collecting several bucketfuls of sediment and finding a spot with the right incline and flow, I begin sluicing. By mid-afternoon, after the rain begins in earnest, I  quit.

Later, after dinner, when the rain lets up, I'm off along another section of meadow edge, hoping for a buck. Again, nothing except more fresh tracks, but they tell me where to head next morning.

First light, as I stealthily near the place, two antlered deer are spotted. A favorable wind direction and wet undergrowth make a stealthy stalk possible. Occupied with browsing, they don't detect my approach.

Releasing at the nearest buck, the arrow strikes as aimed. Instantly, both deer dash off and disappear. From previous hunts, I know to delay following. Time's needed for a mortally wounded deer to stop running, bed down, and die. An hour later, I follow where they went. After only a hundred yards, one's found, dead.  In dressing it out, I note that the arrow had sliced through its heart.

I drag the deer back to camp and hang it from a nearby tree. The cool wet weather lessens the chance of flies *blowing* it, but to make sure, I wrap it in cheesecloth. A medium-sized three-point, it figures to dress out at about 120 lbs.

Noon, and having forgone breakfast, I prepare a hearty lunch. What better than slices of fresh deer liver rolled in flour and fried with bacon, onions, and mushrooms, plus a biscuit and mug of tea?

Next, I'm off in search of a grouse for dinner, this time east of the meadow into a section of forest I hadn't been to earlier. It soon becomes obvious that here's where Mr. Hicks felled the trees he used in constructing his house and other structures. Scattered stumps are everywhere.

There's also a large pile of sawdust where the felled trees were bucked-up. Then, projecting in places from the pile, I catch sight of scattered large rodent-gnawed bleached bones, including a human skull. Shocked, I realize they're almost certainly those of Mr. Hicks.

What caused his death? Was it an accident, possibly from a falling tree, a heart attack, or, after losing wife and son, had he committed suicide? There's no way of knowing.

Finally, the question of why so many of their belongings remain is answered.

That evening, in pondering the day's events, the thought crosses my mind that since Mr. Hicks had used a sluice, he must have met with success, and his cache may somewhere be hidden. Others may already have found and carted it away, but the chance it may still be here merits a thorough search.

In figuring where to concentrate my efforts, I decide my time can best be spent among the old house and adjoining structures. If it's somewhere there, I have an outside chance of finding it. Anywhere else, and the chance is virtually nil. So that's where I'll search, even taking several days if needed.

The next two days are painstakingly used in trying to discover a hiding place among the collapsed boards and beneath the flooring at the old barn, then in and about the tool shed, and finally the root cellar. No luck.

A half-day is spent looking high and low in the house's attic, and another half-day in the rooms below. Floors are thumped, walls and ceilings pounded, and everywhere is probed for a hollow sound or hidden recess. Still nothing.

The house's mortared base of river rocks and the mortared rocks that comprise the fireplace and chimney are possibilities. They're also a last resort. With evening at hand and about out of places to look, while examining a section of chimney inside the house, I notice that the mortar securing one of the chimney's large rocks is more like mud than mortar.

Prying around the edge with my knife, the mud easily chips away. This loosens the rock, and I'm able to lift it away. Behind where the rock had been, a foot square cavity is revealed. Within the cavity are a dozen small leather bags full of nuggets. *EUREKA*!

Because the bags are moldy and crumbling, I scrape them carefully into a bucket, half filling it.

Replacing the rock, I return to camp exultant with the discovery. After an invigorating swim and a well earned dinner, I slide into my tent for a contented night of sleep.

The next morning, again hiding the sluice, I load the cart with the deer, the bucket containing Mr. Hick's cache, and my gear, and head to my car. The cart enables everything to be hauled in a single trip.

Thus ends what unquestionably has been my most bracing visit yet to the old homestead, although, because of bones and skull, another tinged with sadness.

# *Chapter Five*

Back in Bellingham I decide that safe storage of Mr. Hick's cache has first priority.  After removing the moldy leather bags and subtracting the bucket's weight, measured on my bathroom scales, its weight is 53 pounds. At $300 an ounce, after allowing for impurities, that means the cache likely is worth at least $225,000.

That it actually could be worth that much amazes me and starts me thinking.  The cache may not rightfully be mine.  If there *are* living relatives back in Tennessee, they may have claim. But, are there any, and if so who and where are they, and what is their relationship. Unless Hicks fathered other children before he came to the old homestead, he had no other descendents, since both his wife and son are buried at the old homestead.  One thing's certain, I need to carefully think through the ethical and legal ramifications and decide on a proper course of action.

The next day, after putting the cache in a better container, I rent a safety deposit box at the bank and stash it away.

Next, I go to one of the law profs for advice.  So as not to raise questions, I decide to be a bit disingenuous.

"I'm considering writing a novel and need advice on how to handle a certain situation involving the main character. As plotted, the main character has located a large cache of gold nuggets an old prospector had hidden before the prospector and his family was massacred by Indians. What are the main character's ethical and legal responsibilities with respect to the cache?"

What he tells me is pretty much what I'd already surmised. "The finder should do his best to locate any living descendents and, if found, inform them of the cache and turn it over to them. If none are found, the cache belongs to the finder."

The next challenge is to see if there are any living descendents. For an answer I go to the city offices and ask a clerk, "How should I go about locating living descendents in Tennessee of a man about whom all I know is his last name, the full name and birth year of his wife, and approximately when they lived in Tennessee."

After a brief discussion and a check of their files, the clerk suggests I write or telephone the Tennessee Office of Public Records, and gives me an address and telephone number.

About a month after mailing an inquiry, I receive a reply reporting that, based on what I provided; they were unable to find anything. The information I'd given was insufficient.

With that reply I feel that as a practical matter, and for the time being at least, I've tried my best to learn of any living descendents. Nevertheless, because by some turn of events more may someday be learned about the Hicks family, I wouldn't feel comfortable using any of the cache. So I decide to retain it indefinitely in the safety deposit box. If a real need were to arise, I'll decide then what to do. In the mean time, I'll rely upon sluicing to get by.

Realistically, I recognize that although sluicing may be possible for years, its promise could end overnight if others learn the stream has gold. Then, the idea of checking the U. S. mining laws occurs. Possibly, I could stake a claim along the stream that would keeps others out. It's something I should have thought of when I first discovered the stream has gold. And since the nuggets are washing down from somewhere further up, there must be a mother lode. Therefore I need to locate it and stake a claim there as well.

I learn that the Bureau of Land Management is the place to inquire, so I drop by the local office and speak to a clerk named Dale Tingey.

"I plan to pan for gold along a stream that flows across national forest lands and wonder what the laws are governing placing a claim if any gold is found?"

He tells me, "The General Mining Act of 1872 governs prospecting and mining for precious minerals, including gold, on federal public lands." He then hands me a statement BLM has prepared for inquiries such as mine. It reads:

*Under the law, all U. S. citizens 18 years or older have a right to locate a lode (hard rock) or placer (gravel) on federal lands open to mineral entry, and may lay claim to the lode or placer by placing stakes and then registering the claim with the local county clerk and the BLM.*

"Forest Service lands are open to mineral entry." Dale says.

From this, it's apparent I mustn't delay staking a claim any longer. The clerk gives me the necessary paperwork and a booklet of instructions.

While at the BLM office and using a wall map, I point to the meadow area and ask Dale whether a claim may already have been staked. After checking their records he tells me, no.

Figuring that if in all these years no claim has been staked, probably nothing's going to happen in the next few days, so I thank Dale and take the paperwork and instructions back to my apartment to study.

A week later I return to the old homestead and place stakes along each side of where the stream enters and leaves the meadow, four stakes in all. This, after submitting all the necessary paperwork for registering the claim with the local BLM office, as well as with the county clerk. Thus, I now have formally claimed exclusive right to *work* the stream along where it crosses the meadow.

While with the county clerk, I ask whether her records show anything about whether title to the old homestead had ever formally been claimed. After checking, she replies, "We have no record the land was ever owned by anyone other than the U S Forest Service."

With those important details resolved, I'm better able now to concentrate on other matters. I have a special date this evening with Leah, another student majoring in Ecology. She's also completing her senior year, but is several years younger, having entered college fresh from high school.

She's a fetchingly pretty blond of the same Scandinavian ancestry as my own. The first time our eyes met, a bond seemed to form, and for the past year we've been studying and spending ever more time together. As well as having similar intellectual interests, we find that we're *kindred spirits* in other important ways. In fact, our relationship has progressed so that we're talking about tying the knot. It's no longer a question of whether, but only when. Her family lives near Vancouver, British Columbia, and I've gotten to know and like them, as I believe they have me.

Both of us have been giving a lot of thought to our plans after graduating and getting married. She wants to teach, and I've decided to go on to graduate school. The idea of her teaching while I continue with my schooling is a natural, so that's what we decide on as we finish our senior year.

Although I've told her about the side canyon and old homestead, and that the little stream has steelhead, I have yet to say anything about the gold. Over dinner at her apartment while enjoying venison cuts, I finally fill her in about my claim and that so far I've collected nuggets worth almost $30,000. I also tell her about Mr. Hick's cache, my futile efforts to locate descendents, and my intention to let it sit.

Surprised at all she's hearing, she pauses while it sinks in, and then asks, "And why, sweetheart, have you waited until now to tell me?"

Defensively, I explain, "Before meeting you, the old homestead had become a sort of secret escape for when I needed to get off by myself. I tend to be a bit of a loner at times. With the discovery of gold, I became even more guarded. I'm remiss at not having confided in you sooner. From here on out, we're in this together. I can't wait until you see all that's there."

Still a bit unmollified, "Anyway, thanks for letting me know and for bringing me into the fold."

Early in June, after getting our diplomas, we drive to the side canyon, and with backpacks full of camping gear and enough food for a week, make the seven mile hike. Beforehand, I'd checked with the Forest Service and been told their flyovers had found no further signs of marijuana activity.

Leah, because she and her parents are outdoor types and experienced hikers and campers, doesn't need to be taught camp-craft. Together, she and I've spent many days explored some of British Columbia's phenomenal back-country, so I already know of her outdoor aptitudes and skills.

When she catches her first sight of the meadow, framed in forest and surrounded by spectacular snow-capped peaks, she's captivated. The old homestead also catches her fancy, as does the potential for trout in the stream. She quickly perceives, too, that the pond is perfect for swimming.

With it being too early for steelhead, grouse hunting, or mushrooms, Leah and I are left with plenty of time to sluice, explore the surrounding countryside, and simply luxuriate in being alone together amidst one of the region's more beguiling locations. Her enthusiasm for the same things that are important to me convinces me all the more that she's one-of-a-kind and that our relationship is something very special.

After we set up camp, she takes the fly rod and proceeds to catch and clean four small trout for dinner. While she's doing that,  I retrieve the sluice and ready it for use tomorrow.

That first night, as we lie awake in our tent, we're lulled to sleep by serenading coyotes.  Climbing out the next morning and surveying the surrounding scene, she spots six elk in the meadow.  I'd already told her that the area is a virtual wildlife preserve, with elk as well as deer and black bear and even cougar.

After breakfast we go to the stream where I demonstrate use of the sluice.  With both of us working, during several days we fill a jar with about four pounds of nuggets worth maybe $18,000.

"I can't believe that in only three days we've collected that much worth of nuggets.  It's almost enough to see us through an entire year. This definitely is going to take some getting used to!"

"I agree, even now I have a hard time appreciating all it means."

I've been giving further thought to searching for the mother lode. However, because the foliage along the stream is so dense and the terrain so craggy, finding it is bound to be time consuming and difficult. But, with so much at stake, it must be attempted, if not now, eventually. The best way will be to sluice *ever* further upstream until nuggets cease being found, and figure the mother load is nearby.

I explain about the mother lode and the need to locate it. We spend parts of the next few days probing upstream hoping to find where the nuggets stop. Because the going's so difficult, we only cover a half mile, and still there are nuggets. And since, according to my topo map, the stream extends at least another five miles, it's almost certain the search will neither be quick nor easy, or something we'll be attempting any time soon.

The problem, at least during the foreseeable future, is that Leah and I are tied down with more pressing matters. Even though there's the risk others may beat us finding it, it's a risk we must take.

We're constantly together that summer, with time spent with her parents in British Columbia, and also fishing various Northwest steelhead rivers. While already a competent trout fisherman from camp-outs with her family, Leah has never fished for steelhead. It only takes catching one for her to be as smitten as I with their size, strength, and fighting prowess. She can't get over that such large fish come so readily to such small flies.

Also, that summer, she lines up a teaching position in a Bellingham middle school, and I'm accepted in graduate school at the college.

Early in September, with the blessings of her parents, Leah and I are married at their home in British Columbia. After a short honeymoon in Vancouver, we return to the side canyon for another week of the usual activities, including sluicing another $12,000 worth of nuggets. Generous amounts of time also are allotted for romancing beneath the stars.

By late September, we've rented a small house near where Leah's to teach and I attend graduate school. With the nation at peace and prospering, each of us with a degree and happily married, and money in the bank, we can't help feeling good about the future.

# *Chapter Six*

A master's degree generally requires two years, one of classes and the second researching and writing a thesis. During my years as an undergraduate I'd become more interested in and attracted by the *policy* and *political* implications of the environment, than by it as a field for scientific research. So that's where I wish my focus to be in my graduate efforts.

During a meeting with the professors who will be overseeing my graduate work, I express this wish. I also say I'm hopeful of someday making meaningful contributions in ways that will help protect the environment, and trust that my graduate work will help me develop the necessary skills.

They agree with slanting my classes and the focus of my thesis effort  primarily toward *policy* and *politics*, and tell me that, while it'll be up to me to develop the desired  skills, they'll keep that in mind as they work with me  toward my MS.

During my high school and undergraduate years I'd received good grades and earned the respect of my teachers and classmates who, I sensed, looked on me as a role model and leader, qualities I found came naturally.  I figure my loner tendencies also are a plus because they give me more freedom to call things as I see them and act in ways my instincts tell me are right, rather than voicing or doing what's popular or politically correct.

Leah was raised a Methodist, while both my parents were Lutherans, but neither of us had been able to embrace the beliefs and dogma those faiths professed. While having attended church when young, we eventually lost interest and drifted away. In high school, after being exposed to the scientific way of thinking, the concept of evolution began making sense to me, as it had to Leah.

Both of us are entranced by the wonders of nature and have fallen under the spell of the out-of-doors with all it has to offer, and we agree that *the natural world actually is our religion*. We've found that, for us at least, not having to knuckle under to the traditions and practices of a particular faith makes more sense and is a lot simpler and more straightforward.

Nevertheless, we agree that the various faiths have been and are a continuing source of much good, and indispensable to all those people who depend upon them as beacons of guidance in their lives. Only, neither Leah nor I have felt a need for that kind of beacon, and to pretend otherwise would be hypocritical.

Early on in our relationship, the two of us began

attending Unitarian services together at a nearby congregation in Bellingham. We'd learned that the Unitarians are good people who meet to discuss philosophical questions and current events and to perform public service, and that a belief in a Heavenly Personage, while professed by many, isn't a necessary criteria for attendance. We know that when we have children that they will benefit from the kind of broad-minded association such attendance provides, just as we know that our having attended church services as youngsters benefited us.

The school year progresses happily, with Leah engrossed in teaching science at her middle-school, and me laboring under a heavy schedule of graduate classes and looking ahead to next year when I'll be doing field work and writing a thesis.

After careful thought and discussions with my professors, it's agreed that my thesis project is to be an evaluation of the Skagit and Sauk Rivers as units in the National Wild and Scenic Rivers System under Forest Service administration.

The act creating the national system, passed by the Congress and signed by the President in 1968, designated the Skagit and Sauk as two of the initial rivers in the national system. The intent is that the rivers are to be maintained in essentially the same condition as they were at the time they were designated. In other words, the *status quo* is to be continued. Both rivers were assigned to the U. S. Forest Service because it administers most of the lands across which they flow.

I find the thesis project personally appealing because the two rivers are near Bellingham, and because I'm well acquainted with each from years of having fished along them with my father, and later after his death.

In June, following the end of my spring semester and Leah's first year of teaching, and after checking with the Forest Service to make sure no marijuana shenanigans are underway, we head to the old homestead. Our plan is to spend enough time sluicing to finance the coming year.

It had been a winter of heavy snows, so the stream is still gushing water, but that doesn't stop our sluicing or catching enough trout to eat. We also devote time exploring more of the surrounding countryside, including hiking the five miles up to where the stream originates at several small springs near the side canyon's head. From that high up we're able to gaze south and view the summit of Mount Baker. Every day we see deer and elk. We even catch sight of a bear. As usual, coyotes voice their presence.

At night the air is pure and clear and the sky is filled with stars. I know how to locate the North Star by using the Big Dipper, but that's about all I know about the heavens, while marveling at the immensity. One of Leah's hobbies has been learning the names and being able to locate the various planets, stars, and constellations, so it fascinates me to stand with her in my arms as she points particular ones out and explains how they came by their names.

Having learned that the Milky Way is but one of innumerable galaxies in the universe, convinced me long ago that with all the mega-millions of stellar bodies, life in one form or another has to be present many other places besides Earth.

The sluicing goes well and after several long days the two of us accumulate six pounds of nugget-laced sediments worth about $25,000, enough to support us another year. We also plan to get back in September, prior to my returning to school, for more of the activities we've come to cherish, and to bag a deer.

Between now and then I intend touring the Skagit and Sauk rivers to get an even better on-the-ground familiarity with them, as well as to meet with the two district rangers responsible for looking after them as units of the National Wild and Scenic Rivers System. The one having the Sauk is stationed in Darrington, and the other having the Skagit in Sedro Wooley.

In scouting the rivers I find that many sections are readily available from nearby roads.  I note newly built river-side cabins in places, others under construction, and large-scale logging operations underway on adjacent lands.  The status quo, obviously, isn't being protected. Instead, it appears to be business as usual.

In separate meetings with the two district rangers I'm struck by their apparent incomprehension of what wild and scenic river status means, and their indifference to the kinds of protective management the act intends. I mention, "About all I see that's being done is placement of a few signs designating the rivers as units in the national system.  When I ask, "Why isn't more being done to protect the rivers?"  One merely shrugs, and the other replies,  "We don't have the time."

I was tempted to tell them that protecting the rivers wild and scenic qualities seems to be more an annoyance than something to take seriously.  As I later learn, it's good that I didn't.

What *is* plain is that preparing and writing my master's thesis is going to be challenging.  I need to get with my professors to lay out all I've learned from visiting the rivers and talking with the two district rangers. That will be first priority after returning to college and beginning my second graduate year.

In hopes, perhaps, of being able to lease the old house because of its location adjacent to my claim, we make a short visit in late September to see whether making it reasonably habitable appears feasible. We decide it is.

# Chapter Seven

In meetings with my professors, they are only mildly surprised at what I tell them about the seeming lack of action to protect the Skagit's and Sauk's wild and scenic qualities, and the apparent indifference of the two district rangers.

While plotting with them the direction my thesis work should take, I suggest, "Why don't I write to the chief of the Forest Service to tell him about my thesis work, and inform him of my findings to date and see what he has to say?"

One professor responds, "Could be the lack of action you're finding with the Skagit and Sauk is symbolic of other rivers in the national system."

Another ads, "Find out what's being done to protect other designated rivers."

There's agreement that I should query both the Senate and the House of Representatives as to their wild and scenic river expectations, as well as the Secretary of Agriculture who has jurisdiction over the Forest Service, and the Secretary of the Interior whose agencies oversee many of the other rivers in the national system.

They counsel that the job of protecting rivers, while similar to that of protecting national parks or wildlife refuges, probably is a lot more difficult to carry out due to the complications surrounding rivers, with multiple land ownerships, and because rivers play such a vital part in so many ways for the people living along them and/or depending upon them.

"Perhaps the two district rangers simply haven't as yet had time to grasp their responsibilities, much less figure how to live up to them. Perhaps, also, funds in sufficient amounts aren't being provided to implement the intended management and protection," one professor offers.

Another cautions, "Before proceeding you need to get a better idea of the big picture and where everything fits. Don't do anything that will alienate the Forest Service or the two district rangers any more than you already may have done. You're going to have work closely with them and rely on their help as you move forward with your thesis."

In reining me in, as time proves, the professors had it right. I spend the first semester of my second year finding out the problems attendant with river protection and how other river managers are faring in living up to their responsibilities. I learn that the concept of river protection is indeed controversial and complicated, and that the funds and manpower needed to properly do the job have been slow in reaching the actual managers.

In the case of the Skagit and Sauk, while the Forest Service has overall responsibility, there are multiple other jurisdictions involved, including the state, several counties, and Indian tribes. Also, much land through which the rivers flow is in other than Forest Service ownership, including miles of riparian lands in private ownership. So, as my professors had accurately foretold, I find the task of protecting rivers is a lot more complicated and difficult than I at first had thought.

In replies to my letters and in meetings and conversations with various government and congressional officials, I get a more comprehensive understanding of the big picture. I also realize how fortunate it was that I never did blow the whistle on the two district rangers. Instead, my second semester is spent working closely with them in formulating a comprehensive long range plan on how the rivers can best be managed and protected and what it will take in the way of funding and manpower.

That plan, plus all the background obtained from everyone I've been in touch with, comprises my thesis, which is completed in draft form and submitted to my professors in October. Following further sagacious help from them, it's approved, and I receive my Masters of

Science degree.

The whole exercise has been an eye-opener and given me valuable experience in problem solving, public relations, writing, and other skills that will be essential if someday I'm to take my place in helping to achieve significant environmental protections.

The professors are happy with the way I went about the field work and with the resulting thesis, and encourage me to apply to major universities for a scholarship leading to a PhD, saying they'll send letters of recommendation. Both the Department of Agriculture and the Department of the Interior apparently impressed with my efforts and the thesis, advice me to take the necessary Civil Service exams to qualify for an appointment with one or another of their agencies. Even my congressman, Bob Dennis, with whom I'd conferred and kept apprised of my efforts, offers me a position on his staff in Washington DC.

Leah and I are eager to move to the next stage in our lives, but there's no hurry. While I intend finding work soon, our sluicing is continuing to provide enough to tide us over, and we still hope eventually to locate the mother lode.

During the summer while I was writing my thesis, Leah had inquired about leasing the old house. She learned that under the terms of the General Mining Act of 1872, leases may be granted in connection with placer claims. So, we submit the paperwork and in due course a lease is granted for as long as the placer claim remains active.

Visiting the old house that autumn, we make a list of everything that'll be needed to make it actually habitable. Among other things, a thorough top to bottom cleaning, the roof re-shingled, some exterior siding replaced, windows and doors repaired or replaced, furniture added, and back-country implements provided. Our plan is to acquire all that's needed to accomplish the work, bundle it together in Bellingham, and then truck it there next spring.

With the archery season in progress, Leah gets a three pointer. She had hunted with her father in British Columbia and taken a couple of deer using a rifle, but never with bow and arrow. Before heading out on her own, I describe where and how two years earlier I'd taken my deer, and the place and circumstances of hers are almost identical.

"I'll bet you never thought I'd get one, did you?" she joshes, after returning to camp for help in dragging it back, "and it's even dressed out!"

Now that I have an MS, several employment

opportunities present themselves. The Nature Conservancy needs a manager for its holdings along the Skagit River. It's acquired more than 3,000 acres of river-frontage, and has plans to acquire more as lands become available and they find the money. Bald eagles swarm the river during winter to feed on spawned out salmon, and TNC has an ongoing long range program to help safeguard them.

The College needs another Ecology teacher.

Becoming our congressman's local representative and heading up his office in Bellingham is another tempting possibility. I'd become acquainted with Bob Dennis while doing my thesis, discovered that we have similar political philosophies, and we hit it off. After I'd declined joining his staff in Washington DC because of our wish to remain in Bellingham, at least for the time being, he'd kept me in mind and now offers me the position.

Leah and I consider the various options and then decide that I should sign-on with Bob Dennis. He's a Republican, a dedicated environmentalist, has been elected to six terms, and appears a cinch for more. There's good pay and the opportunity to get lots of valuable experience. The position won't begin until after the first of the year, so Leah and I have time to gather all we need for the old house in preparation for trucking it there come spring.

My job with the congressman proves even more interesting, challenging, and valuable than I'd anticipated. As well as manning his Bellingham office with the help of a secretary, I'm his eyes and ears locally. In his absence, which is most of the time, I represent him at meetings and preside at others for the purpose of learning the views of his constituents on matters they care about and he has under consideration.

We get together when he flies out about once a month, and in May he has me come to Washington DC for a week to get to know his staff and see how they operate. He serves on several important committees and has his hand in a wide range of matters that keep everyone on his staff hopping.

A minor down-side with the position is that because of all the work it entails, Leah and I have less time for steelhead fishing and side canyon activities. However, we manage to squeeze in a few days here and there, and because we both relish our busy lives so much, neither feels deprived.

# *Chapter Eight*

As soon as weather allows that spring, and after obtaining permission from the Forest Service to use the road and getting a key to the gate, we truck everything to the old house. Two trips are needed because there's so much.

Although my new job keeps me busy, Leah and I find time to accomplish all that we've planned.    First priority is thoroughly cleaning the inside rooms and attic, as well as repairing and painting them.  Next, the roof is re-shingle and funky exterior siding replaced, as are several windows and broken panes in others.  A new front door is installed.  The foundation, fireplace, and other stonework are re-calked where needed. The old stove is cleaned and repaired and its chimney replaced.

Outside, using pipe found the marihuana growers hid, a system for bringing water by gravity flow from a nearby spring into the house is installed. Finally, out back next to where the old outhouse had been, a deep pit is dug and new outhouse erected.  The newly dug dirt is used in filling the old pit.

Most of the work is accomplished over a two week period by college students we'd become acquainted with, including the four I'd earlier met when they hiked in and stayed overnight. Either Leah or I are on hand during the two weeks to pitch in and oversee.

With all these changes, the insides have been made reasonably impervious to pack rats and weather and the house is again livable. No longer is it necessary to tote a lot of gear in every time we come, or to live out of a tent.

That the Forest Service has retained the entrance gate to prevent vehicle traffic by marijuana growers and others, suits us fine. We enjoy the hike up and back, and know the gate dissuades all but the occasional backpacker or hunter. By locating a few *No Trespass* signs in the vicinity of the old house and *Keep Out* signs on the house, visitors are made aware that the place is actively in use.

Up to now, most of our sediment collecting and sluicing has been along the meadow between the four stakes I'd set when the placer claim was filed. While additional sediments continue washing down, they no longer are replenishing as fast as we're using them in our sluicing. Consequently, we're finding ever fewer nuggets. So we've begun spending more time sluicing above and below our claim. It's more difficult because of all the brush, but necessary if we hope to continue collecting the $25,000 in nuggets each year we've set our sights on.

We foresee the day when sluicing will be so

unproductive as to hardly be worth the effort. But that appears to be some years ahead, and in the meantime what we sluice, plus what we earn in our jobs, guarantees a comfortable income. And, eventually, locating and exploiting the mother lode remains a possibility.

Neither of us has revealed anything about the placer claim, so the only others who know are in the offices where I filed. We assume they consider it privileged information, but who knows. With the price of gold fluctuating between $300 and $350 an ounce, there hasn't been enough incentive to get people out prospecting. But if the price increases enough, we could end up sharing the stream with others.

A self-perpetuating population of trout continues providing sport and meals. Steelhead reliably ascends to the pond, with others likely in secluded brush covered pools.

One concern is that bears could break into the old house. We're careful to burn our garbage and never leave food scraps about, and we board up the windows and reinforce the door when leaving for the winter.

We've discussed the possibility of starting a family, but with both of us so busy, decide to hold off a few more years. Leah is still in her mid-twenties.

Manning the congressman's Bellingham office and

representing him on numerous occasions in and about his district and the state results in my becoming increasingly well known. Leah, a popular middle school science teacher, also is getting exposure. We hone our speaking, writing, and public relation skills, and relish the challenges that come with our jobs.

Although not being overly active socially and neither playing golf, we've become friendly with other young upward-mobile Bellingham couples, including Bob Dennis and his wife Marge when they're in town, and get with them for dinners, picnics, and other socials. We also regularly attend Unitarian Church services and find the broad-ranging discussions stimulating and worthwhile.

With the College close by where we live, we make a point of attending the lectures and musical programs it attracts. I've retained close ties with my old professors and with former students who attended with me. The Ecology teachers sometimes have me speak to their classes on subjects relative to my work with Bob Dennis or my training as an ecologist.

And, whenever Bob Dennis is in town, he invariably is invited to address various town gatherings and meet with faculty and students at the College, tasks he enjoys and at which he excels.

# Chapter Nine

**W**hile at the old house early the next summer, two visitors approach. They're dressed in hiking gear and have small packs so, from a distance, we assume they're merely out for a walk. When they get closer, one looks familiar. He's Dale Tingey, the BLM clerk I'd filed my placer claim with several years earlier. He remembers me, too. After acknowledgments, he introduces his companion, Bob Cameron, another clerk in the same office.

They seem friendly enough and Dale says, "We had a day off and wanted a hike and thought this would be an interesting place to go."

We invite them in and show what we've done to again make the old house more livable and other structures more useful.

Leah's in the middle of preparing a meal, so she invites them to join us, but with plans to head further up the canyon, they decline.

Dale says, "Thanks for showing us around. We've never been here before and, remembering you'd staked a claim, were curious."

Instinctively, their visit bothers me. Sure, they merely may have wanted a hike, but then he mentioned my claim.

The price of gold recently has been on the rise and currently is about $400 an ounce. Could it be that since they know of my claim, they're considering filing one of their own? In discussing it with Leah, she tends to agree there's more than meets the eye in their having hiked here at this particular time.

Of course, there's nothing to preclude others from filing in the side canyon, something I'd recognized and been relieved hadn't happened. But, perhaps our solitary use of the area is about to end. If we encounter them again, or learn they've been in the vicinity, they probably intend to file.

As Leah and I still are nowhere near being able to devote the time it would take to locate the mother lode, even though it now would be the smart thing to do, we're forced to wait and see what happens.

Then, during a July visit, when we find stakes downstream about a mile from our claim, I decide to do a little checking on the two. Working for the congressman, I had gotten to know the BLM district manager, so I telephone and ask whether any of his staff have filed the claim and mention the two who had paid us a visit.

The next day he calls to tell me that while none of his staff has filed a claim, a close acquaintance of the two has, and warns, "He isn't someone you want as an enemy. He has a reputation as a trouble maker. Twice he's been arrested for breaking and entering, and twice more apprehended for poaching deer. He even served a short jail sentence."

Then, in August, I happen upon a young man standing along the stretch of stream I'd staked. In talking with him, he reveals he's the one who filed a mile downstream. I tell him a little about my claim, and ask how he's doing with his.

"I'm finding a few nuggets, but the stream is so hard to get at because of all the brush, it's been very slow going. I envy what you have here, now that I see what it's like."

He seems friendly enough and nothing like the 'trouble maker' the district manager had portrayed. When he leaves, we shake hands, names are exchanged, and we commit to staying in touch. His name is Tom Strike. No mention is made of his two BLM friends.

Later that summer the BLM district manager calls again to say that he'd felt it necessary to terminate two of his employees. "The reason I gave was that they had prompted a close acquaintance to file a placer claim based on *privileged* information." He told me they were the same two I had mentioned earlier, Dale Tingey and

Bob Cameron.

Hearing this, Leah and I get our heads together and, figuring the two and Tom Strike are in cahoots, consider what might be done to forestall possible trouble, or at least a source of friction and worry.

My always sensible wife suggests, "Let's try to defuse the situation. Assuming all three will be working the claim, can't we somehow demonstrate we don't resent their activity, show an interest in how they're doing, and offer to be of help." And she then suggests, "Why don't we try hiring the three of them to search for the mother lode?"

"Leah, what a great idea; if they find it, we could share the claim. I'd even go along with splitting it four ways, with each of them owning a quarter, and us a quarter. That's overly generous, but we're running out of time and the risk is increasing that someone else may beat us to it."

A close acquaintance of ours is an attorney, and when I tell him of the situation and how we propose handling it, he advises, "Yes, it would be possible to enter into a binding contract that prevents them as your employees from filing, and would legally allocate the results four ways, once the mother lode were found. All four parties would need to agree and sign the contract."

He then drafts a contract for us to use in the event the scenario plays out as hoped.

Mid-September, when we park near the mouth of the side canyon, a pickup truck rigged to carry three motorbikes already is parked. Around one end of the locked gate are tire marks. Six miles up are a tent and three motorbikes. Nearby in the stream, Tom Strike and the two ex-BLM employees are hard at work panning.

As Leah and I approach, while not belligerent, they don't seem overly cordial. When we appear friendly and pleasantly ask whether they are having any success, and show interest in how they're going about it, they ease up a bit.

Tom Strike speaks up. "We're finding a few flakes and an occasional nugget, but its hard work and we're not getting as much as we'd hoped."

From their body language, it's obvious the three are discouraged.

Leah asks, "We're on our way to the old house and plan on being there for a few days. Why don't you join us for dinner tomorrow evening? We've found using a sluice is a lot more effective than panning and could show you how it's done."

With Leah's positive approach, their manner moderates. They readily accept the invitation.

"We'll look for you about six. Okay?"

In making this trip, we had anticipated having the three join us and possibly begin winning them over, and we knew that a really good meal would help, so we planned with that in mind.

Next day, Leah gets busy and soon has a delicious mulligan stew simmering on the stove filled with potatoes, carrots, peas, onions, tender chunks of venison from her last year's buck, plus chanterelles we'd collected earlier in the day. While she's busy with the stew, I get to work preparing a salad of lettuce, tomatoes, onions, avocado, radishes, and blue cheese dressing, plus watercress from a nearby spring. A pan of rolls warms in the oven.

When they arrive and see what awaits them, their eyes light up and their mouths water. They're long overdue for exactly the kind of hearty meal we've prepared. No doubt, they haven't been eating all that well and can't wait to join us around such a bounteous table. They'd considerately brought a six pack, which only adds to the conviviality.

In between bites, Dale and Bob tell of losing their BLM jobs, that they haven't as yet found other work, and that they plan to remain that autumn in hopes of finding enough gold to make ends meet. Tom says that he's an auto mechanic, but currently unemployed, and that he too plans to continue working the claim. None is married

We tell them something of ourselves, and that we make it up several times a year to fish and hunt and collect mushrooms, as well as to sluice. We say we're having some success sluicing and that while its hard work we find it an enjoyable and a profitable way of spending a few hours.

After a companionable and utterly satisfying meal during which we sense a good rapport is forming, we take them to the stream and demonstrate how to go about using a sluice. They're impressed when, after a little practice, several small nuggets are found. We then give them one of our sluices, saying we're building another.

Leah and I are eager to see how things work out with the three, now that the ice is broken. If a solid relationship develops, as now looks to be happening, we'll broach the possibility of contracting with them to search for the mother lode

Leah and I lay plans for us to get together with them some more that winter in Bellingham to further cement our relationship.

# Chapter Ten

Twice in the succeeding months we have the three in for dinner. We learn that after they'd built two additional sluices, they began getting better results, and although the dense brush still makes sluicing difficult, they're eager to resume again next spring.

During the second dinner, and after Leah and I believe a solid relationship and sense of trust has formed, we tell them about the mother lode possibility farther up the canyon and our hope of someday finding it. But that right now we're too busy with our careers to seriously undertake the search.

I ask, "Would you three be interested in spending time searching for the mother lode? We would like to contract with you to do so, and would pay a generous hourly wage. If you find it, we would share the proceeds, with each of you owning a quarter, and the two of us a quarter."

Leah adds, "You realize that because of the tangled undergrowth and difficult terrain, the search almost surely will be time consuming and arduous, and it will take you away from your sluicing."

Each appears interested. Tom asks, "May we give it some thought, and then let you know?"

"Sure, there's no hurry. Field work won't be possible until late spring after the snow melts and the stream becomes workable."

Leah and I had decided to offer each $10 an hour for time actually spent on the ground searching, to extend through the coming field season, for a maximum of no more than 500 hours or $5,000, each. We figured that if the mother lode were to be found, it should happen within the amount of effort that time-span provides. We also figured that by spring the three will be too much in need of money for them to risk heading out on their own looking for the mother load.

A few days later Tom telephones for more details, including what the pay would be and how long it would last, which we tell him.

The next day he calls to say that they've decided to do what we're proposing. "We figure that the search probably will pay better than what we could get sluicing, plus the deal you're offering is too generous to refuse."

So, together with them and our attorney friend, a contract is signed.

Leah and I reluctantly decide that we'll borrow from Mr. Hick's cache to pay the three, because $15,000 appears to be more than we can afford right now. If by the end of the field season the mother load isn't found, we'll do some extra sluicing to repay whatever's borrowed. If it *is* found and mining it proves profitable, we'll repay from our share.

Leah continues to enjoy her teaching, and I'm extra busy helping to gear up the congressman's campaign for reelection the coming November.

Several times that spring and summer we get to the side canyon and find the three hard at work and making good progress, as they progress up the stream. In early September Tom telephones and elatedly reports that they've finally found where the stream no longer has nuggets. He says it's up near where the stream originates. He also says a small side gully meets the stream at that point.

Leah and I visit the site with them and spend half a day confirming their findings. We agree that the side gully almost has to be where a gold-bearing vein of quartz lies and the nuggets originate.

Cold weather and snow prevent further work that year, but plans are made for them to begin prospecting up the side gully as soon as weather permits next spring. We pay the three a total of $14,400 for the 1,440 hours they had jointly logged. The three seem genuinely appreciative.

As it turned out, Leah and I were able to sluice

enough that summer and autumn to meet our own quota, plus covering the amount we paid the trio, so it wasn't necessary after all to borrow from Mr. Hick's cache.

Leah pitches in that autumn to help with the congressman's reelection campaign. He's been a caring and effective representative, is popular, and wins handily. He again asks me to move to Washington DC, this time to head up his staff. I tell him, definitely later, but not right now. He and his wife had joined us once for a visit to the old house, so he knows of our claim. When I reveal that it appears we're close to finding the mother lode, he understands our temporary reluctance to move east.

Tom and the other two eagerly await being able again to resume searching. One of the most gratifying circumstances of working with the three has been seeing them getting their lives back together. Each is more up-beat and shows increasing confidence and enthusiasm, especially Tom Strike, the one with the troubled past and reputation as a troublemaker.

The possibility that one or another somehow might take advantage of the situation lingers, but nothing happens to prompt concern. Nevertheless we monitor their activities and the results they report.

Tom is the leader and spokesman and Leah and I

have taken a strong liking and have regularly begun inviting him over for meals or just to socialize. We're curious about his past and, while not pressing him to reveal anything, hope in time that he'll volunteer information. After being with us several times, he opens up.

"I live with my mother and a younger sister in a little house on the outskirts of Bellingham. My father was a logging truck driver, but he deserted the family many years ago, forcing my mother to be the bread winner.

"When I was about sixteen, I began getting spare jobs to help out, because the family was really struggling. During one spell, none of us had enough to eat. That's when I began sneaking into homes hoping to find jewelry and money. Twice I was caught and after the second time I was sent to a reformatory for two months.

"It was during that spell I also was caught poaching deer. The family was so desperate and I had only wanted to help. With time to think in the reformatory, I finally realized where that kind of behavior was heading, so after getting out, I trained to become an auto mechanic."

Leah and I detect that Tom possesses unusual

qualities, and are willing to overlook his past derelictions as acts borne of youthful desperation. Tom in turn has come to regard us as friends, and looks to us for companionship and advice. He tells us that if the mother lode is found and proves profitable enough, he plans to go to college and become a lawyer. Leah and I determine that if the mother lode doesn't work out, we'll see that he gets his education.

That spring, as soon as conditions permit, the three head up the side canyon on their motor bikes, along with a tent and camp gear. They set up in a small meadow near the side gully. Our contract has been renewed and continues paying them $10 an hour, refundable if the vein is found and mining it proves profitable.

Water intermittently washes down the gully as snow melts and rain falls. It's this action over the years that's eroded the gully and uncovered the vein (assuming its presence). As the vein's exposed, the flow of water breaks pieces off and carries them into the stream, where they wash below.

The three lay plans that winter about how to proceed. They'll methodically begin clearing brush and pick and shoveling their way up the side gully, all the while keeping an eye out for where a vein of quartz with traces of gold breaks the surface.

"I'm all but certain it's there," I tell them, "and very confident you'll soon locate it. Once it's found and if the vein is rich enough, we'll file a lode claim in accordance with our contract.

# Chapter Eleven

The gully extends sideways from the stream for about 600 yards. Over a period of three weeks of very difficult brush clearing, pick and shovel work, and searching, and after progressing about a third of the way up the gully, a vein of quartz containing flashes of gold *is* located.

The three are elated, as are the both of us. Samples are chopped out and brought to Bellingham for analysis. The amount of gold in the samples, while small, is definitely of commercial quality. Immediately, a lode claim is filed and the five of us are in business.

I get with Eric Bedard, a local mining engineer friend, tell him about our find, and invite him to go to the gully. After reviewing the sample-analysis results and carefully inspecting the site, he advises, "You'll need to begin tunneling along the vein. The prospects are exciting!"

He then asks, "Would you be interested in contracting with me to oversee the operation? It will mean trucking ore to a refinery, which will require making the old road passable. We'll need to hire an experienced miner and use tunneling equipment. There also will be mine tailings to dispose of in an environmentally acceptable way, and special measures taken to make sure the stream isn't polluted. All of which I'll arrange and cover, if you'll guarantee me half of whatever is grossed.

"From the quality of the samples and what I've observed at the site, I'm quite confident the endeavor will be nicely rewarding. However, as you know, the vein could play out after only a little tunneling. But, I'm willing to take a chance, if you are."

"Eric, that sounds to be just what's needed, but I'll have to discuss it with the others.

First I go to a teacher friend at the College's business school who happens to be familiar with the kind of arrangement Eric has proposed. He thinks the proposal is reasonable and gives me a copy of the sort of contract to use.

Leah and I then meet with the other three, explain Bedard's proposal and what my business school friend said, and recommend that we accept. They agree, and a contract with Bedard is signed.

By late-summer Bedard has secured all the necessary permits, improved the road, hired an experienced miner, and is hauling out one truck-load of ore a week. The operation is soon grossing $75,000 a month.

In the interest of causing the least possible environmental disruption, we decide to work the mine *only* while the road's free of snow and passable, which extends over a period of about six months. That results in a yearly gross of about $450,000, half of which goes to Bedard. The other half, divided four ways, comes to about $56,000 annually. Even if the vein plays out after only a few years, the remuneration will be substantial.

Tom Strike makes a down payment on a better home closer to the center of town, and moves there with his mother and sister. His mother no longer needs to work full time. He also enrolls at the College with expectations of a law degree after the required number of years. The other two, once again having found employment, look forward to a brighter future.

Leah and I, while already financially self-sufficient, welcome the additional security and independence the mine affords. We have no immediate plans to change the direction of our lives, and intend to continue with our jobs, with the prospect before long of moving to Washington DC for two years.

And, of course, we continue fly fishing northwest rivers for summer steelhead, and using the old house, now comfortably refurbished, as a base for enjoying all the back-country activities that have become such an important part of our lives together.

The locked gate across the side canyon's mouth remains in place, but as long as the mine is in operation, the Forest Service permits those with business there to have keys. The weekly ore truck is a distraction, but it's something we gratefully accept.

The next summer, during one of our visits to the old house, a young man, after backpacking up the road, comes to our door and asks, "Do you know anything about an old settler named Byron Hicks who moved west from Tennessee back about the turn of the century? He may have homesteaded somewhere nearby, maybe even here? He was my great grandfather."

Nonplussed, I respond with an emphatic, "*Yes, please come in so we can talk!*"

Over dinner we learn more about the Hicks family, and about the young man who tells us his name also is Byron Hicks.

"Ever since I learned that my great granddad had come west, I wanted to know more about where he went and what happened to him. Finally, I decided the best way to find out was to come west and actually try to locate where he settled. Because the letters he'd written home were saved, I was able to trace him here."

Leah and I then tell him how we come to be here.

How I'd ventured up the side canyon some years earlier hoping to find steelhead, camped in the meadow, and discovered the stream had gold. How after learning that no claim had ever been filed for ownership of the land and it now was part of the national forest, I'd filed a placer claim along the stream, and we'd leased the old house.

I also tell of learning that a couple had occupied the meadow about 1910, but no one could recall their names, and then of finding the two gravestones with names and dates, and of the scattered bones and skull now stored in a box in the attic.

"My father's the son of one of the two sons my great granddad left behind when he left his wife in Tennessee and headed west," Byron relates. "Quite a few of his descendents still live in Tennessee. No one knew that he had taken up with another woman because it was never mentioned in his letters."

After dinner we show Byron the two gravestones, and the bones in the attic almost certainly those of his great grandfather. We also invite him to remain overnight.

The next morning he joins us for breakfast prior to heading back to where his car is parked. "I plan to drive to Bellingham, and should get there this evening."

"We plan returning later today and would enjoy having you in for dinner and more talk," and give him our telephone number. "Also, what's your address in Tennessee, just in case we don't manage to connect?"

We'd said nothing about the *cache* because we wanted first to learn more about young Byron and to try to verify his story.

Returning to Bellingham and after several telephone calls to Tennessee, I reach Byron's father who confirms everything his son had told us about himself and the circumstances of his great grandfather having come west. I also telephone Will Hammond, my lawyer friend, tell him about Byron, and ask his advice on what to do about the cache.

"Inform Byron of the cache, how you had tried unsuccessfully to find descendants of his great grandfather, and how you had then deposited the cache in a safety deposit box. Then, take him to the bank and show him the cache, and suggest that since the gold rightfully belongs to his great grandfather's direct descendents, he needs to telephone his family and learn what they wish to be done. The logical thing would be for them to direct Byron to sell the cache and arrange for the proceeds to be transferred to their bank in Tennessee."

The following day Byron calls and then joins us that evening for dinner. While we're eating he tells us more about his family and himself, including that he's twenty-one and in his third year studying history at Tennessee State University in Nashville.

After finishing our meal and moving to the living room, I inform Byron of the cache, the circumstances of my finding it, and that it presently is in a safety deposit box at a local bank. Not unexpectedly, he's astounded, especially when he hears that it may be worth $300,000.

I relate how, after writing to the Tennessee Office of Public Records with the little I knew about his great grandfather and requesting the names of any living descendents, they'd replied that I hadn't given them enough information for them to be of any help.

"The cache rightfully belongs to your great grandfather's descendents. We never used any, figuring a descendent may someday turn up, just as you've done.

"Also today, I asked the advice of an attorney friend. He says you need to inform your family about the cache and find out what they wish to be done. What he suggests is that they have you sell it and then transfer the proceeds to the family bank in Tennessee."

Leah adds, "After you talk with your family, we'll help any way we can to arrange whatever they decide."

Still astonished, Byron says he'll telephone his family and then get back to us. The next day he tells us his family wants him to do as the attorney suggests. So we go with him to the bank, he retrieves the cache, and after having it carefully assayed, sells it.

Because the price of gold recently has spiked, the cache's value assays at $420,000, and is sold for that amount. The Hicks family, after generously insisting that we accept a finder's reward of $50,000, soon receives a cashier's check in the amount of $370,000, as telegraphed to their bank in Tennessee.

"My family is reasonably prosperous," Byron says, "but the money is sure to be well spent, probably in helping young family members get an education."

We tell him of our sluicing, the enjoyment it provides, and that it's been a big help in getting us on our feet and keeping us solvent.

"This is my first visit west. After seeing something of California about which I've heard so much, I plan to leisurely make my way back home."

We give him some ideas about what to see in the Golden State, as well as advising him to get there by way of the scenic highway down the Pacific coastline.

"Keep in touch Byron, and next time you're out, plan on spending some time with us at the old homestead," Leah invites.

What we didn't know was how soon our paths were destined to cross again.

# Chapter Twelve

Leah and I feel right about the caches disposition. It's where it belongs. While there'd been some comfort in knowing it was in the safety deposit box, I was never tempted to use any of it, other than the possibility of *borrowing* to help pay the three to search for the mother lode, a need that never materialized. I suppose, in the back of my mind, I'd decided that what eventually did happen was going to happen.

And then, that autumn, we receive a disturbing call from Byron Hicks.

"My first cousin, the son of my father's brother, has been stewing after learning of all the money the family received and has decided to go out there and check things out for himself. His name is Rudy; he's twenty-four, a bit of a hot-head, and very impulsive. I'm afraid he may cause trouble! The family tried to talk him out of going, but he was determined, and already is on his way by auto."

I thank Byron for letting us know and tell him we'll just wait and see what happens.

A week later Rudy Hicks telephones to introduce himself and to say that he's in town and wants to learn more about his great grandfather and the old homestead and would like to meet with me. I arrange for him to come to my office the next morning.

As I'd anticipated from what Byron said, Rudy is *aggressively* determined to get results.

"Byron filled me in on what he did while he was here," Rudy asserts, "but I want to go to the old homestead and see what's there for myself. I've already been to the BLM office to find out about your placer claim and your lease on the old house."

I'm tied up for a couple of days, but arrange to take Rudy to the old homestead on Saturday. Early Saturday morning, Leah and I pick him up at his motel and make the sixty minute drive. I want Leah along so she can meet him and take his measure. She's a good judge of people, and I want to be able to compare notes.

Using our key to the gate, we drive to the old homestead. After escorting Rudy around the general area and pointing out the section of stream I'd filed on, we show him the house, where the cache had been, the two gravestones, and the bones of his great grandfather.

In answer to a direct question, I reply, "Yes, we're doing some sluicing, but the results are private."

Rudy is surprised that the house is in such good condition, so we tell him that we'd repaired and renovated it so we can use it whenever we come for a few days, which we usually do several times a year.

"If my great grandfather settled here, didn't he have title to the land, and didn't he file a placer claim on the stream?" Rudy asks.

I figure he already knows the answers since he's been to the BLM office, but reply, "When I first came here I had the same questions, but when I checked with the BLM, Forest Service, and county clerk, I learned there's no record of anyone ever having held title to the land, or of having filed a placer claim, and that the area became part of the national forest when it was established many years ago."

Rudy noses around by himself for another hour, and takes numerous photographs. Finally, satisfied with what he's seen, heard, and done, he tells us he's ready to return to Bellingham. On the drive back he continues grilling us about the old house, the cache, and our placer claim, as well as our future plans for the place, without revealing any of his own intentions.

A few days later, Mike Sawyer calls. He's a reporter with the local newspaper. "I'm preparing an article about old Byron Hicks and his homestead and would like to interview you to corroborate information that his great grandson, Rudy Hicks, already has given me. And I'd like to learn more about the old homesteader and the place where he once lived."

This catches me completely unawares, but I reply, "Yes, I'll help any way I can."

So he comes by my office. "Rudy Hicks," he says, "came by our offices after spending time at the old homestead with you and your wife, and is urging the newspaper to do an article."

He then proceeds to relate what Rudy told him.

All I can do is corroborate most of what Rudy had said, while clarifying minor details.

Mike says, "There's a lot of human interest in stories like this and my editor has assigned me to prepare a major spread. He plans to run it in next Sunday's edition."

This is disconcerting because we've revealed almost nothing of our involvement in the old homestead, of the placer claim, of finding the two tombstones and bones and skull, or of finding the cache and turning it over to the Hicks family, all of which Mike's gotten from Rudy and plans to include in the article he's preparing.

When the lode mine began operating, it was reported in the newspaper and is common knowledge locally. While with us, Rudy had brought it up, but when I told him it's unrelated to the old homestead, he didn't make it an issue in his conversation with Mike. However, it's sure to be mentioned along with everything else in the newspaper article, since the newspaper already has a file on it.

What Leah and I can't fathom is Rudy's purpose in going to the reporter and instigating such an article, and what he intends to gain. He already knows we acted in good faith in securing the placer claim and lease, and that his great grandfather, while occupying the land for a period, never actually held title nor filed a claim. Plus, we certainly had demonstrated our good intentions by holding onto the cache and then turning it over intact to the Hicks family. All we conjecture is that he's a born *troublemaker*, enjoys putting others on the spot, and hopes for some obscure reason to cause distress or embarrassment.

It's with some anxiety that we open up the Sunday edition. There it is, everything laid out. The article even includes photographs Rudy snapped while he was with us at the old homestead.

The following morning the police call to ask why we haven't reported the tombstones and bones. The local historical society calls to ask what right we have to occupy the old house, and whether we've compromised its historic integrity. Bob Dennis calls from Washington

DC to find out what all hullabaloos he's hearing is about. And people we've never known, as well as quite a few we do know, stop us on the street with questions.

I'm interviewed by the local TV station and for the next several evenings fifteen prime-time minutes are devoted to the subject. About all I can do during the interviews is to parrot what's contained in the newspaper article and say that we have nothing to hide and never saw any point in making a splash of our activities.

The story has legs for a few weeks, and in due course the police quiz me about the gravestones and bones, the local historical society visits the old house, and next time I talk with Bob Dennis he laughingly tells me to ignore the ruckus.

Rudy Hicks neither shows up again nor contacts us further. Neither, to our knowledge, does he follow up on anything, so we assume he's merely slunk away, content with his deviltry.

Byron Hicks telephones to find out whether Rudy ever showed up and, learning he did, has me fill him in on all that happened. I also mail a copy of the newspaper article.

Two weeks later, Byron calls again to bring us up-to-date. "Rudy's returned and has almost nothing to say about his visit there. Knowing Rudy as well I do, that means nothing worth crowing about happened, so rest easy."

I tell him, "We had nothing to hide and we weren't too worried, only puzzled."

As the old adage goes, all good things must come to an end. Well, our involvement in the old house didn't come to an end, but there are changes. The local historical society informs us that while we may continue to use the old house, our status is more as caretakers than lessees. I learn that they'd tried to get it formally declared a state historic site, but because of our repairs, it didn't qualify.

The mine continues to produce for three more years, but then, when the tunnel is almost a quarter-mile in length, the gold laden vein of quartz begins to play out and soon ends. Eric Bedard tells me we're lucky the vein ran as far as it did. So the operation is terminated, the tunnel sealed, and the site restored. But not before it had lasted almost six years and, because the price of gold continued increasing, each of the four partners banked almost a half million, and Bedard netted close to a million.

With the mine shut down and road no longer in use, the gate at the mouth now has a new Forest Service lock. This is okay because having to again hike in keeps us in shape. It also dampens visitation by others, although a few more than before make the hike because of the newspaper article.

As we knew to expect, our sluicing efforts keep resulting in ever fewer nuggets. We continue, but more because it's relaxing and pleasurable than remunerative, even though the price of gold keeps climbing.

There's still the usual abundance of trout and steelhead, as well as mushrooms, grouse, deer, and elk, and coyotes continued entertaining at night. No wolves or grizzlies yet, but from all we're hearing and reading, it's only a matter of time.

# BOOK TWO.  PROGRESSION

## Chapter Thirteen

Jim Murrow, another teacher in Leah's middle school, has been investing in stocks for several years and enjoyed some success.  Lately he's been following an emerging new company in particular, *Microsoft*.  He knew Bill Gates and Paul Allen, the two entrepreneurs, having attended Lakeside School in Seattle with them, and is gleaning everything possible about their efforts to start up the new company.  He's intrigued by what he's learning and excited about the company's prospects.  They soon plan an IPO, at which time the company's stock becomes available for sale to the public.

Leah and Jim are friends and he shares his enthusiasm for the two founders and their new company and ignites an equal amount of interest in her.  Both decide the company is going places and that as soon as the stock becomes available they should invest.

"Pete, Jim Murrow, the gym teacher at my school, attended Lakeside School down in Seattle and got to know two other students who he says are geniuses. They're into computers and have invented a system of software that will make computers useable by anyone. They recently started up a new company they call Microsoft and the word Jim has is that it's a sure winner. They're about to issue an IPO and begin selling stock. He plans to buy as many shares as he can afford, and urges we do also. What do you think?"

"Well, I don't know much about the stock market, but I'd be willing if you think it's a good idea. What do you suggest?"

"Sweetheart, as you know, I've been following the market for some time and it looks to me like computers are about to take off. Based on what Jim tells me and what I've found out on my own, I believe we should take a chance."

"We have the $50,000 the Hicks gave us. Why don't we invest half? Even if it doesn't turn out as great as Jim and you believe, we probably could resell the shares and recoup some." All along we'd intended someday using the $50,000 to help buy a house, so it'll be a change in our plans.

"Okay, it's a gamble, but I believe it's one worth taking. As soon as there's an IPO, I'll buy $25,000 worth and we'll just see what happens."

The first day the stock comes on the market Leah and Jim each invest at $29 a share. Our $25,000 buys

860 shares. It isn't long before the stock takes off and begins splitting and it's apparent that Jim and Leah had the right idea.

Even before Microsoft, we've been making a comfortable go of it. Therefore, rather than cash in any of the shares, we merely list them with Fidelity and sit back and wait.

The next time Bob Dennis is in town, he again asks me to move back and head up his office in Washington DC. Appreciating our feelings for the Northwest, which are much like his own, he promises, "It need only be for two years. You'll both find lots to interest you back there, and the experience will be invaluable in the event you someday decide to run for office. I'm giving some thought to running for the Senate; if that happens, there's no one I know that's better qualified to replace me in the House."

Late that winter, we make the move. Because I have five years experience running Bob's office in Bellingham, plus having gone back there each year for short visits, I have a good understanding of what the job entails. We rent an apartment in Arlington, Virginia, just across the Potomac River from Washington DC and only a quick subway commute to his office.

Neither of us has ever resided for any length of

time outside the Northwest, other than my three years in the Army. Leah soon is hired by another congressman as a legislative assistant, so both of us quickly become immersed in life on The Hill.

I have my hands full directing a staff of half a dozen members, as well as assisting Bob while he participates in the various committees he serves on. Leah, too, spends a lot of time in committee work, both in researching pending legislation and attending hearings. Both of us enjoy watching the political bigwigs in action, including occasionally even the President.

As Bob had said, the East and especially the environs around the nation's capitol offer much to see and do. Time permitting, we attend Watergate concerts and visit many of the region's historic sites. We also get to the beautiful mountains of Virginia and West Virginia, and to the Maryland and Virginia seashores. Another staffer in the office likes to canoe and takes us on camp-outs along several of the area's scenic rivers, including the upper Potomac and the Cacapon. Free tickets to concerts and lectures are available to staff members, as well as invitations to exclusive parties at the various embassies and plush lobbyist functions.

Between our duties on The Hill and our efforts to

see and do as much else as possible, we're kept going week days and even weekends. It's a rat race, but an enjoyable and rewarding one.

After two years and with my replacement already on board, we're ready to return to Bellingham and resume the kind of life we both cherish. Since we'd been able to return once a year for two weeks, we haven't been completely deprived, but there's still catching up to do.

When Bob asks, I agree to head up his Bellingham office again, but there are several months from when we leave Washington DC to when I begin in October. Leah again has signed on to teach at the same middle school, also beginning in October. That means both of us are free for several months before again having to hunker down.

Our first task is to buy a house. We have the $25,000 remaining of the finders reward money, plus much of what we realized from the lode claim operation, and with both of us having been working there is more than enough to acquire and furnish a comfortable house, which we soon do. Our Microsoft stock that continues gaining in value and splitting, is left to ride.

While East, I was hearing and reading that steelhead fishing in Washington has been on the decline. Visiting favorite rivers, we find that to be so. We catch a few, but it's nothing like it once was. Could it be that our technique has become a little rusty, or is it because there are fewer fish and more fishermen? The explanation, we decide, is the latter. Other anglers we talk with agree.

We drive to northwest British Columbia in September and spend two weeks angling some of that area's fabulous steelhead rivers, including the Skeena and its Kispiox, Morice, and Bulkley tributaries. A friend, who's familiar with the rivers and has a boat, meets us and takes us where he knows there are fish. That makes the experience a lot more productive than if we'd gone there cold. The rivers offer wonderful sport, but no better than we'd formerly known in Washington and Oregon.

We savor being able to return regularly again to the side canyon and old house. It's about the same as when we left; only the local historical society has erected a marker which tells of the old Byron Hicks family and describes the workings of his homestead. The stream doesn't disappoint. It's still full of trout, and the pond continues harboring steelhead. Sluicing, while no longer generous, remains enjoyable. The archery season is one of our last outdoor activities, and I get a prime four pointer.

We learn that wolves and grizzlies are about, probably strays from nearby British Columbia.

Therefore, we're alert for signs. That some are around only adds to the area's *mystique*. We don't see any wolves, but twice we hear them howling at night. Possibly, a pack's taken up residence.

# Chapter Fourteen

We've been away for two years, but because of our deep Northwest roots it doesn't take long for us to get back into the swing of things.

In recognition of my long interest in the out-of-doors and the environment, as well as my high profile with the congressman, the Governor asks if I'll accept an appointment to the nine-member Washington Fish and Wildlife Commission. The Commission is responsible for setting policy and overseeing operations of the state's Department of Fish and Wildlife.

Before deciding, I check with Bob to see if he has any objections. It will mean spending a fair amount of time carrying out Commission responsibilities, leaving less for my duties with him. He says to go ahead.

I figure I'm suited to the position because of my experience as an angler and hunter and my training in ecology and the environment, so I accept the appointment.

Commissioners, as well as knowing the way the Department operates and something about the various resources it manages, must learn and understand the views and concerns of the public-at-large. Each interest has views of its own that must be taken into account and weighed in order to strike a fair balance. In addressing those views, the Commission schedules public meetings about a dozen times a year throughout the state.

As a commissioner representing a part of the state where salmon and steelhead are paramount, I hope to focus my efforts in halting the alarming decline in native salmon and steelhead runs. My duties may also involve the growing numbers of wolves and grizzlies in my part of the state and the possible effects they may be having on big game and livestock.

Because of all my years angling for steelhead and my close tie-ins with other anglers, I already have some idea of the reasons for the declining runs. While realizing there are multiple reasons, two appear the main culprits. One is that dams now straddle some of our largest and what once were the most productive rivers and either block or hinder the ascent of fish to critical spawning beds.

The other is that vast tracts of forest have been denuded by over-aggressive logging, with little consideration given the resultant effects on rivers and fish, something I know about first hand from seeing it happen along the Skagit and Sauk.

Another possibility is the effect the state's massive hatchery program may be having on native salmon and steelhead runs.   Rather than being the panacea for rescuing fish runs lost to dams and logging, what I'm now hearing and reading is that it's another of the culprits.   Hatchery fish, by cross-breeding with natives, are destroying the genetic diversity that has enabled the natives to utilize all the various riverine niches.

There's also a disquieting rumor that the Department may be staffed with employees who instead of taking the lead in saving the native runs, may actually be hindering if not impeding what should be happening.

After I've been with the Commission for going on three years, I'm finding the demands of being a commissioner, added to those of managing the congressman's Bellingham office, are depriving me of essential family time.   Therefore, I decide to give up my job with the congressman.   As well as freeing up time for the family, I'll be able to concentrate more in helping rescue the endangered runs of native salmon and steelhead.

I tell Bob about the dilemma and my decision. He understands and asks only that I stay on until he finds a replacement.   He also reminds me again that I'm the one to replace him in the House if he runs for the Senate.

Up to now I've never said anything to Bob about my religious beliefs.   Maybe it's time.

Leah opines, "Sweetheart, if you ever make a run for public office, the issue is almost certain to surface. Why don't you tell Bob what you believe? You two have such a good relationship and he's such a sensible guy, see what he has to say."

A few weeks later while Bob's in town to break in my replacement, we get together for lunch. When he again mentions the possibility of my running for his seat, I respond, "If I were to run, people almost surely would want to know my religious beliefs, and I'd have to tell them I'm an *atheist*. Wouldn't that end any chance I might have of being elected?"

"You may have a point, Pete; you've never said anything, and I've never thought to ask."

"My parents were Lutherans and I regularly attended church when I was young, but with an in-borne inclination to question, some science classes behind me, and after a lot of reading and careful thought, I finally rejected the idea that a *Heavenly Personage* is directing everything."

"Pete, my views are quite similar, but to be elected I've sidestepped them. When I invoke the word '*God*', the meaning to me is more that of an 'all-powerful force', than a Heavenly Personage. Actually, I've never offered my views, and never been asked. If it were to happen, I suppose that would be my reply."

"Interesting, Bob, because it's almost the way Leah thinks. She rejects the idea of an actual Heavenly Personage, but falls short of claiming she's an atheist because she believes there has to be an *Intelligence* orchestrating the way the universe came into being and works, that it couldn't simply all be randomly happening.

"Doesn't it fly in the face of a country founded on the premise of religious freedom, that one can't admit to being an atheist and have any chance of getting elected to public office? After all, while religious freedom guarantees the right *to* believe in a God, it also should guarantee the right *not to* believe."

"Yes, Pete, and one of these days that attitude may change, but don't hold your breath. Neither the Constitution nor the Bill of Rights require a belief in God, or even include the term God. In fact, Article VI states, "no religious test shall ever be required as a qualification to any office". All that stands in the way of atheists being elected is the sacrosanct religious fervor that's so prevalent.

"On the other hand, isn't it fortunate that so many have a belief in someone they trust and can turn to in times of need?"

"I agree, Bob, it's best that most earnestly believe

in a Heavenly Being and subscribe to an established religion with its tenets to guide them.

"If the question ever arises, I'll probably say something to the effect that I believe some yet to be fully understood laws of Physics are in control, similar to what Einstein began postulating. The laws of Nature also play a part."

"That may sail Pete. It certainly will be interesting to see what kind of a reaction it provokes. We may find out if you decide to run for office."

# Chapter Fifteen

The Dean of the College's Political Science Department, Ike Armstrong, someone I'd often interacted with while serving with the congressman, invites me to lunch and asks, "Would you be interested in teaching a class or two within my department dealing with environmental politics? It's a subject I feel needs teaching and I know it's something you are well versed in and care about. I have a number of case studies you could use."

Two years have elapsed since I left the congressman, and I'm finding myself with time on my hands and rather at loose ends. My duties as commissioner, once I'd settled into the work, were proving to be less demanding than I'd supposed, and remembering all the challenging and interesting work in the congressman's office, I was becoming a little bored.

What Ike offers also would help fill the coffers which suffered when I gave up working for the congressman. So I answer, "Ike, I'm really tempted. Let me give it some thought."

Leah has sensed my boredom, so when I tell her about the offer, she eagerly advises that I accept. She also has an announcement to make.

"Pete, you remember several years ago that we decided there was no hurry in starting a family, well my doctor informed me today that I'm three months pregnant." She's now thirty.

Catching her in my arms, I exclaim, "Darling, what wonderful news, I couldn't be happier!" and tenderly plant a kiss. Then, with a wink, "I'm only surprised it hasn't happened sooner."

To celebrate her announcement, we go to the town's best restaurant for dinner. Now that both our lives soon are to change rather dramatically, with her stopping teaching and becoming a mother, and I begin teaching and becoming a father, there's much to consider about where we now are and what lies ahead.

While eating, our conversation, as might be expected with two people so in-tune, is relaxed and for the most part lighthearted.

We reminisce about the side canyon and the old house and homestead, all the happy as well as unusual memories they evoke, and how the placer and lode claims have changed our lives.

Leah teases, "And remembers all the arm twisting it took for me to get you to pony up for the Microsoft stock? What's its multiple now? I'll bet you don't even know, or care?"

"Okay, okay," I jibe with a smile, "but it took Jim to put you onto it, remember, and without the twenty-five grand you filched from our house-buying account, it wouldn't have happened."

Leah, then, "I assume you already know that Tom recently passed the bar and plans to hang his shingle here in town. Nice we could help."

"I feel we really did help. I know he's grateful, and now he has a lot going for him." Tom's become a close and valued friend and we regularly get together for meals, talk, and trips to the side canyon.

"He and Sally are soon getting married. You know her; we've been with them a few times. She's that cute teacher at my school. I introduced them."

"Yeah, she's a doll. Glad your efforts to *tether* him finally are paying off."

After soup and salad, I think out loud about my commissioner job. "It looks as though our friends in Olympia may be giving in a little on hatcheries. I only hope it's not too late. And the bill on wolves and grizzlies is stuck in committee; no surprise there. Until a bunch of sheep are slaughtered, or somebody gets hurt, nothing's likely to happen."

We're both ever mindful of the marihuana growers. "Thank goodness the Forest Service is keeping a wary eye. I'm pretty sure they'll stay away."

Leah, nodding, "Maybe the growers have given up, but you never can tell. Unfortunately, they're only the tip of the iceberg. What's hurting the country is the hard stuff."

I agree, and the conversation drifts into a lament about other things that have gone wrong, seemingly in just the last few years.

Leah, "You know, sweetheart, that movie we decided *not* to see the other night? It's been ages since I've heard of one I'd ask you to take me to."

"You've got that right. Hollywood is all about Hollywood. No surprise it's struggling, with all the *garbage* it turns out. The last flick we saw---don't even remember the name it's been so long---I had to close my eyes during some of the sex scenes. Really crass. And I'm not that old, either! The entertainment industry in general is a disgrace. Once, it set the tone for the way people should behave and for civility. Now, it's all coarseness and vulgarity."

Leah sighs, "Well, at least we have a choice with TV, one need only switch channels or zap it."

She then bemoans the music scene, something she rues a lot. "Oh for another Rogers and Hammerstein, or Lerner and Lowe. I know musicals and plays still are being written, but nothing's happening that even comes close what those people regularly turned out. Why is that?"

"Probably it's a generational thing; cultural standards are slipping and there's a lot more to distract those who normally would be writing and composing the kind of stuff we enjoy."

Leah's eyes narrow. "You're right there. We mentioned Microsoft earlier. The electronic world is becoming so sophisticated, and so lucrative for the *whiz kids* who get in early. I fear *that* world is drawing way too many of our best and brightest away from the things that really matter."

In seeing someone buying lottery tickets from the restaurant cashier, I'm reminded of another angst. Motioning for Leah to look, I tell her, "We know that gambling *hooks* people, just like drugs. And now by selling lottery tickets, the state no less is encouraging people to gamble. What does that tell you?"

With the recital of things gone wrong, what mostly had been a cheerful occasion, has turned into something more somber. Leah, sensing it needs rescuing, remarks, "Despite all the negatives, we have it pretty good. I can't help marveling how blessed we are to have been born, brought up, and be living in the Pacific Northwest, with all its fascinating places and marvelous outdoor opportunities."

"Yes, there's no place like it. Washington and Oregon are wonderful and British Columbia at least as great as I've come to appreciate from outings with your family. And don't forget Alaska---we soon must take advantage of its world class fishing."

Over desert, as the evening winds down, our talk ends on a positive note as we happily look ahead to the expectations and challenges awaiting us as new parents.

The next day, I drop by Ike's office. "Leah is as enthusiastic as I am about my teaching in your department, so count me in."

"Great! I'm sure you're going to like teaching, and with all you have to offer I'm confident your classes are sure to be a valuable and popular addition to our program."

Ike had mentioned *a class or two*, but since teaching will be something new to me, I opt for only one at first. "Okay," Ike says, "we'll see how it goes before deciding about a second. What I have in mind is a five-credit-hour class, which means you'll be teaching about an hour a day, Monday through Friday. Is that doable?"

I pick up the case studies Ike had mentioned and begin going through them for ideas. I also talk with several teacher friends at the College for advice on how a new teacher with no experience gets jump-started. During my years with the congressman I'd gained a lot of exposure speaking before groups and in leading discussions. It was something I enjoyed and came natural, so I figure standing before a class won't be a problem. I can't wait to begin.

When the list of autumn semester classes is released, it states that Pete Eckland will be teaching a five-credit undergraduate course entitled, 'Environmental Politics'.

Nine o'clock, first Monday in October, finds me standing before 25 eager bright-eyed students. After introductions and some good natured back and forth banter to achieve a little familiarity, I tell them something of our subject matter, what the class work will include, and what I'll be seeking to achieved by the time the semester ends. I also inform them what I'm expecting in the way of effort.

# *Chapter Sixteen*

Teaching agrees with me, and I sense my students appreciate what they're learning. With the case studies Ike provided, plus others I found, there's no dearth of teaching material. Depending on how complicated the subject matter, I decide that to do a case study justice, three or four class hours are needed, plus a lot of outside student reading.

Our first case study is my master's thesis. I distribute copies for the students to read, and the class then reviews the political process by which the Skagit and Sauk were added to the National Wild and Scenic Rivers System and the role played by the Forest Service. On field trips to both rivers, the students meet with the two district rangers and learn firsthand about their management challenges. We then talk about and consider the students' observations and opinions. When finished, they have a good understanding of the Act creating the national system, the politics involved in selecting the two rivers, and all the complicated issues the Forest Service is dealing with in carrying out its legislative mandate.

Another case study pertains to the establishment of Olympic National Park. During a field trip to the

Olympic Peninsula, the students see the contrast between the magnificent old growth forests within the park, and the dreary logged-over clear-cuts and tree farms outside. It's a *vivid* comparison. They meet with the park superintendent, as well as Forest Service, DNR, logging company officers, and tribal leaders for Q&A sessions. A particularly interesting and enlightening aspect was the epic political struggle that ensued leading to the establishment of the National Park in 1938.

By the time the semester ends, the class has dissected and evaluated twelve case studies and the students have learned about the political implications of a wide range of environmental issues, together with all the pros and cons involved.

Half way through the semester, Leah and I become proud parents of twin boys. I'm grateful she endured a normal pregnancy and birth, and we're both very happy with the results. Although she misses teaching, she settles nicely into motherhood, and with twins is kept busy. We name them Einar and Bruce, Einar after my father, and Bruce after Leah's.

My class has received good grades from the students, so Ike invites me to continue. He also asks, "Do you have ideas for a second class?"

I tell him I do and, having already given it some

thought, suggest, "Ike, there's a serious need for a class that deals with the Earth's most urgent environmental issues. Five I have in mind are over-population, soaring-expectations, pollution, deforestation, and biodiversity. If you have a few minutes, I'll tell you briefly about each and why it's important they're better understood and people begin talking about them."

"By all means, go ahead." He then politely (and I believe interestedly) listens as I give thumbnail descriptions.

"Over-population heads the list. The planet's human population was about one million in 10,000 BC, one billion in 1900, six billion in 1970, and is predicted to be eleven billion by 2050. This *explosion* has come about in large part because of medical advances and advances in food production, but also because of ignorance, chiefly in under-developed countries.

"A second urgent issue is soaring-expectations for an ever higher standard of living by growing numbers of people. Less than a hundred years ago, almost everyone was satisfied with a single *modest* house and auto. Now, most aspire to owning two or more *elaborate* examples of each.

"Unless mankind somehow awakens to the dangers of over-population and soaring-expectations, and disciplines itself to living within the planet's *carrying capacity*, critical life support systems inevitably will fail and everything now being done to protect the environment will prove to be little more than a holding action. Already there are signs that the earth's capacity for sustaining mankind has been exceeded and some life support systems are irreversibly failing.

"Another critical issue is the world-wide *pollution* of air, water, and land. Rampant and irresponsible disposal of waste and contaminates is harming almost all forms of life. Air over most large cities is choked with industrial and commercial pollutants and fumes from autos and other means of transportation. Oceans are receiving quantum amounts of pollution and huge areas are becoming overwhelmed and sterile. Likewise with rivers and lakes. Vast land areas are being inundated with garbage and other disposables, including much that's not biodegradable.

"Yet another pressing issue is the way the planet's forested lands are being logged and converted to other uses. At the current rate, all rain forests will be gone within a hundred years. Loss of forests grievously affects most of the planet's land animals and plants, seventy percent of which live within them. As well as increasing greenhouse gases and global warming, deforestation also causes flooding, erosion, the straightening and steepening of rivers, and a dramatic loss of aquatic life.

"Biodiversity is another vital concern. With *good* biodiversity, the earth is healthy and its ecosystems are able to withstand and recover from catastrophes. With *bad* biodiversity, the earth sickens.

"These issues and others, Ike, have overriding environmental, economic, and political implications that aren't getting nearly the attention they deserve."

"I agree, Pete, students would really gain from a class like that. It also would motivate them to pitch in and help find solutions. Obviously, you know the subject matter. Let's add a three-credit-hour class, beginning next semester."

With two spring semester classes, I'll be humping, but the subject matter is of such overriding importance, I can't resist.

Down through the years I'd eagerly read most books dealing with the environment and mankind's excesses, including such classics as Rachel Carson's 'Silent Spring', Aldo Leopold's 'A Sand County Almanac', John McPhee's 'Encounters With the Archdruid', and Stewart Udall's 'The Quiet Crisis'. And, because of long-time membership and participation in the

Wilderness Society, Sierra Club, and The Nature Conservancy, I'd kept abreast of all the major environmental issues facing the nation and world. So it won't be much of a stretch for me to gear up for the new class.

The spring semester goes swimmingly and the two high profile classes get good reviews and enhance the department's standing within the College. Consequently, Ike invites me to carry on. That suits me fine because it's so vital that more people learn about the subjects. The extra income they bring, while modest, also helps.

Leah and I have settled nicely into parenthood and the twins are beginning to walk. She's joined a great books club that I enjoy attending with her, and both of us are involved in various faculty activities. With no classes to teach that summer and only the normal amount of Commission matters scheduled, we get in some steelhead fishing and make several trips to the old house.

The next few years are almost repeats for Leah and me, personally and professionally. The twins are now in school, Leah's become a substitute teacher to spell other teachers who are sick or on leave, and my two classes have become standard fare at the College.

Word spreads about the success of the two classes and REI adds me to its board of directors, as do the

Washington chapters of The Sierra Club and The Nature Conservancy. And, by invitation from Bill Ewing, Dean of the College of the Environment at the University of Washington in Seattle, I guest lecture several times.

Byron Hicks writes that he's received his MA in history at Tennessee State University and is now a teacher there. Knowing my role at the College, he inquires about the prospects of his joining the faculty? The History Department Dean tells me there may be an opening autumn semester, so I telephone Byron and suggest he send an application.

We've kept in touch with Byron over the years and Leah and I believe he would be a credit to the College. So it pleases us when he calls to say he's been invited for an interview.

Leah meets his plane and brings him home to stay with us while he's in town. Following his appointment with the History Department Dean the next day, he joins us for a visit to the old homestead and an overnight stay in his great grandfather's house.

Good natured, and even enthusiastically, he joins in as we fish, swim, and gather enough mushrooms for dinner. We even do a little sluicing. Relaxing around the kitchen table and savoring Leah's delicious cooking, affords us the chance to reminisce about our life in the

Northwest and to tell him about all the vast region's wondrous attributes. If he hasn't already decided to move here, assuming a position is offered, what we say should make up his mind.

Still around the kitchen table, Byron reflects on happenings back in Tennessee. "The money from the cache is reserved in a trust to be doled out in helping young family members get an education. It even helped me get my graduate degree. Rudy currently is trying to get his feet on the ground after a long bout with *John Barleycorn*, but it isn't looking good."

Mention of his meddlesome cousin evokes a full recitation of the perplexing and humorous chain of events that involved us while Rudy was here stirring up mischief.

After we return to Bellingham and Byron is about to leave for home, he confides, "My interview with the History Department Dean went quite well. He asked me about my background and experience, and told me what he has in mind for the position I'm being considered. He also showed me around the History Department and introduced me to several of the faculty. He didn't commit to anything, but I'm optimistic."

In seeing him off at the airport, Byron laughs and answers the inevitable question from Leah, "No, I'm not engaged, and right now I don't have a steady girlfriend, but as I was strolling around the campus, I couldn't help noticing there's no dearth of pulchritude."

# Chapter Seventeen

Five years have gone by since I was appointed a member of the Fish and Wildlife Commission. During those years I've learned a great deal about native fish runs and the effects that dams, bad logging, hatchery operations, and other disruptive practices have had and are having on them.

The series of dams that make the Columbia River a *staircase* of huge reservoirs, have virtually eliminated the runs of native steelhead that once ascended to its higher tributaries, including such rivers as the Yakima, Wenatchee, and Methow, rivers famous for the numbers and size of fish. What had been the most productive river system in the world for native steelhead is now only a glimmer of its former self. The same can be said of the Cowlitz and other rivers, large and small.

Excessive and badly designed logging operations have decimated thousands of miles of rivers, causing them to flood, straighten, and steepen and destroying much of the potential they once had for fostering healthy native runs.

The Department too quickly subscribing to the idea that hatcheries could successfully *mitigate* the damaging effects of dams, improper logging, and other destructive practices on native fish runs. In its eagerness to alleviate the *short term* effects by relying on hatcheries, it failed to properly assess the *long term* consequences. As a result, countless steelhead runs were lost because of the hatcheries.

The Department is still dominated by the hatchery culture, with more than 80 state hatcheries and others being built   that's costing $50 million annually to operate, and has hundreds of employees and their families dependent for a living. The problem is compounded by dozens more federal and tribal hatcheries

One reason for the present hatchery conundrum is that many of the senior staff who received their schooling when hatcheries were in good repute, still are in denial.   Crimping back the hatchery program will be difficult and will need to be spaced over a period of years, but it must be done if the native runs are to be saved

The rumors I'd heard that Department personnel were dragging their feet and actually impeding actions needed to begin restoring native runs, particularly by senior staff imbued with the hatchery mentality,  turned out to be all too true.

With five years of Commission experience behind

me, I've formed very definite ideas about what's needed to begin restoring the state's native runs.

On each occasion when the Commission meets with the Governor or appears before the state legislature and my views are sought, I emphasize that native steelhead are among the state's most important resources, and that since the state's rivers are at the center of a range that extends all the way from Central California to Alaska's Kenai Peninsula, the state should be providing the region's best fishing, not some of the poorest.

I point out the urgent need for the Department to adopt modern up-to-date management concepts and practices, and to shed the old worn out ones, but that it won't happen until it's adequate funded.

I stress that if native runs are to be saved, the various impediments that have been and still are jeopardizing them must be corrected. They are many and varied, and as well as dams, bad logging, and hatcheries, include ineffective culverts, channelization, riparian developments, pollution, predation, netting, livestock grazing, and coastal fish farms---to name some of the more egregious.

During those years, as I became better acquainted with all the many factors affecting native steelhead runs and the Department's role in managing them, I identified specific actions the Department must begin taking if the runs are to be started on the road to recovery:

- Be more aggressive in promoting the removal of obsolete dams, and in seeing needed culverts are installed and ineffective ones replaced.
- Monitor all ongoing logging operations that threaten rivers and fish runs, see that any infractions are promptly corrected, and firmly insist that all future logging operations are soundly conceived.
- Manage rivers by erring on the side of caution wherever the status of native runs have yet to be determined.
- Along rivers known to have viable runs, make sure that their spawning potential is fully realized.
- Terminate hatchery plants along all rivers known to harbor viable runs.
- Continue hatchery plants only where they are justified by particular circumstances, such as in rivers incapable of supporting native runs.
- Require that anglers release native steelhead on all rivers known to have native runs.

- Where natural obstacles such as waterfalls block migrating fish, either alter the obstacles to permit fish passage, or haul the fish above the obstacles, thus opening up thousands of additional stream miles.
- Emphasize that steelhead are more valuable for the sport they provide, than as food for the table.

In my efforts to rescue the native runs, I realize that accomplishing all I wish to see happen will take years, but believe that with persistence it's achievable. One thing's certain, unless substantive progress is *soon* begun, the runs inevitably are going to continue declining with little chance of ever being rebuilt.

All I've been advocating is critical, but I knew it wasn't going to happen unless *someone* was willing to come forward and forcefully speak out. Early on, I decided to be that person.

Many are in agreement with what I'm seeking, but there also are detractors. My views have become the subject of pro and con newspaper articles and letters-to-the-editor and, as hoped, inspired useful debate.

As with anyone who takes a stand, I've become controversial. However, because everything I'm seeking has merit, I've refused to back down or be silenced.

\*\*\*\*\*\*\*\*\*\*\*\*

In September, Leah's dad, Bruce, invites me to join him hunting moose in British Columbia. He'd been doing it every few years and plans to again this year. He knows an area some distance north where getting a moose is a virtual certainly if one spends a few days, so that's where we head.

I welcome the opportunity because I'm in need of a change and because moose are such good eating. Leah and the twins accompany me to her parent's home where they remain with her mother while Bruce and I hunt.

Bruce hires the guide he regularly uses, and within two days each of us has a moose. After giving away most of the meat, there's still a hundred pounds in our freezer.

Byron Hicks telephones that he's accepted a teaching position with the College's History Department, beginning this autumn. He expects to arrive in about a week, and already has rented an apartment near the campus.

# *Chapter Eighteen*

After three years of teaching environmental politics, I feel that my knowledge and understanding of the subject is sufficiently honed for me to write a text book. When the Dean endorses the idea, I go to several publishers. One expresses interest, but wants to see a draft. Because what I have in mind encompasses most of what I've been teaching and already is down on paper, a draft is soon ready. After reading it, the publisher tells me it has merit and offers to take it on. One of their editors is assigned to work with me and in three months the book is in final form and a first edition of 5,000 copies printed.

While not making the New York Times best seller list, it gets good reviews and is soon a prescribed text at several colleges besides my own. There even are modest over-the-counter sales.

My appointment as a Fish and Wildlife Commissioner is soon due to expire. Because of the strident way I've argued the actions I believe are needed, reappointment is unlikely. Even if asked, I've decided to decline. Everything I've been advocating to shape up the Department and rescue native runs is on the table. More, I believe, can be accomplished from outside.

Leah and I have been giving serious thought to our future. We wish to continue living in Bellingham, or at least in the Northwest, and decide our best prospects lie in my continuing as a teacher, authoring books about the environment, and guest lecturing. However, for me to advance in those fields, means getting a PhD.

Recognizing the advantages, we decide to make the commitment. As Leah puts it, "It's now or never, Pete, no question, we're going to do it!" While costly, by delving into our lode-claim money and maybe even selling some Microsoft stock, we figure it's possible.

I'd gotten to know Bill Ewing, Dean of the University of Washington's College of the Environment in Seattle, while guest lecturing at his invitation. With similar interests, we struck it off, so the next time I'm in Seattle I arrange to meet with him to discuss the possibility of my enrolling in his College and working toward a PhD.

"Pete, that's exactly the right thing to do. I don't know why, with your abilities and accomplishments, you haven't done it before now."

"What are the requirements, Bill, and what's the chance of my doing some teaching on the side?"

"At least a year of graduate classes will be needed, and a dissertation's required. A faculty committee will be assigned to help chart your classes and choose the dissertation problem. They'll provide guidance while you work on the dissertation and pass on the final product. It also will be up to the committee to recommend you for the degree. I'd guess it'll all take about three years.

"With your teaching experience and the success of your classes, plus having published a textbook, lining up teaching assignments within my department won't be a problem."

That will mean my having to take a sabbatical from the College and move to Seattle for at least three years. As for the dissertation, I already know what I want to do and hope my faculty committee agrees.

I finish teaching my two spring-semester classes, the College grants me a sabbatical, we rent out our house, Leah finds an apartment near the campus and enrolls the twins in the same grade school where she's been hired to teach, and we move the family to Seattle in time for me to begin that autumn.

The first order of business is for me to meet with the faculty committee that's been appointed to oversee my efforts. They quiz me about my experience and accomplishments, and then ask what I have in mind for a dissertation. "All too often," I say, "the Congress is quick to designate national parks, wildernesses, wild and scenic rivers, trails, and other such popular federal preserves, but slow to provide the funding needed to make them work. My dissertation will identify all the instances of it having happened, the consequences, and how the procedure might be improved."

After a lengthy discussion during which they offer a number of useful suggestions, they approve the problem essentially as I've proposed. They also help me decide on the graduate classes I'll be taking.

The Dean, a member of the committee, then invites me into his office and tells me that he wants me to teach the same two classes I've been teaching at the College, only abbreviated to reduce the burden on me. I readily agree.

Academia at the huge university is vastly different from what we've been used to at the College, but the family adapts to the new environment and all its challenges.

The classes I attend are taught by well known environmental and political science scholars, and prove to be eye-openers and very stimulating. My dissertation requires two trips to Washington DC for discussions with congressional staffs and agency personnel, and endless researching both in The Library of Congress and other record depositories. After a painstaking critique by my faculty committee and several rewrites, the dissertation is approved. I then meet with the committee for a final evaluation, and they decide in my favor.

Three years after beginning, with Leah and the twins proudly in attendance, I don the robes, ascend the rostrum, and receive a *Doctor of Philosophy*. It wasn't easy but proved to be a most rewarding and satisfying experience.

While most of my efforts and energies were in getting the degree, from what I learned in the classes I took and from the professors I had for teachers, I was able to upgrade my two classes. Both were as well received at the University as they had been at the College; consequently, the Dean invites me to join his faculty as a tenured assistant professor.

With no immediate decision required and an urgent need by the family for some R and R after the rigors of the last three years, we go first to Bellingham to reclaim our house, and then to the side canyon.

The twins by now are able to carry packs and the seven mile hike poses no problem. With all their exposure over the years, they've become as attached to the place as Leah and I.

It's too early for steelhead, but trout are there in

their usual abundance and its fun watching the boys catch them for our meals. They also have become eager sluicers and their efforts plus our own help in a small way to abet our frayed finances.

With my textbook gaining usage, and publication of my dissertation, two other schools offer me teaching positions, one in Oregon and the other in British Columbia. While there wouldn't be quite the prestige or pay as at the University, we're interested because the schools are smaller and the atmosphere more laid-back. Leah and I visit both and are similarly impressed by their faculties, programs, and facilities. The one in British Columbia has the advantage of being close to where Leah's folks live, and only 75 miles from Bellingham.

A fourth option is to return to the College in Bellingham. Because my previous teaching was in Ike Armstrong's Political Science Department, I drop by to pay my respects and see what he might suggest. We'd kept in touch while I was at the University, so he knows of the PhD and that I'm casting about for something to do.

"Pete, I assume you've heard that the College has expanded and become a full-fledged University. Phyllis Redman only recently was selected to be the new President to implement the expansion, and she's already in the position. She's a real go-getter, as well as being a delightful person. I'd like the two of you to meet. May I arrange an appointment?"

That sounds like a good idea. The next day Ike telephones and says the new President wants to meet and would like us to come by at two o'clock. Upon being notified that we've arrived in her outer office, President Redman graciously comes out and ushers us inside. Her friendly upbeat personality and dynamism immediately impress me.

After introductions and general remarks about her recent arrival and plans for the University, she says, "Pete, Ike has filled me in on the excellent teaching you did for him a few years back, as well as all your other accomplishments, including your recent doctorate. As you probably know, the University presently doesn't have an Environmental Department, but we want one. I would like to get it underway this coming autumn semester, and already have added the Department on our roster and reserved office space and classrooms. Would you be interested in organizing and heading it up, including hiring and directing a small staff?"

To say I'm surprised would be putting it mildly. "President Redman, what a generous and exciting offer. Of course I'm interested, who wouldn't be. May I talk it over with Leah, my wife, and then get back to you?"

"By all means, I've enjoyed our meeting. Thanks, Ike, for bringing Pete by. I hope he accepts."

The offer from President Redman is a bolt out of the blue. I'd figured something might be offered, but nothing of this magnitude. There are still the other three offers to consider, each of which is attractive.

Leah and I evaluate the pluses and minuses of all four offers. After eliminating Seattle and Oregon, the decision comes down to either the position in British Columbia or the one in Bellingham. Over the years, both of us have put down Bellingham roots, mine a tad deeper because I was born and grew up there, but when I finally get around to asking Leah the one she prefers, she doesn't hesitate an instant, "*Its Bellingham!*"

Aside from wanting to remain in Bellingham, I admit the idea of organizing and heading a new department is both appealing and attractively challenging. After informing the three other schools that I've decided to remain in Bellingham and rejoin its faculty, I arrange another meeting with President Redman. I want to personally tell her of our decision, as well as learn more about what she has in mind for the new department. I also want her and Leah to meet.

She is gracious as before, and I can tell the two

ladies feel an instant rapport. After the formalities and telling her what we've decide, I ask what she has in mind for the new department.

"Other than a general knowledge of what's needed, I don't have any preconceived ideas, Pete, and would like to get your thoughts. Why don't you think it through and then give me your recommendations briefly in writing. After I have a chance to study them, we can get together and make the necessary decisions."

"That would be perfect, President Redman, I'll get something to you in a few days."

As I'm fresh from the University in Seattle and have first-hand knowledge of the advanced approach its College of the Environment has been taking in environmental teaching and the makeup of its classes, I have a legs-up on what to include in the statement to President Redman. Best to start modestly, and then as the situation warrants, add classes and teachers. Initially, during the first year, one other teacher beside me, plus a secretary, should suffice. The other teacher will handle several classes, while I teach the two I'd earlier taught at the College, as refined at the University.

While in Seattle, I'd become acquainted with other doctoral candidates, a number of whom I judge would make excellent teachers. Having kept in touch, I telephone two, both now graduated. One's already commitment, but the other, Joyce Bennett, is free and looking for work. I tell her that the College has become a University, of President Redman's interest in starting a new Environmental Department, and what my role is to be. When she says she's definitely interested, I promise to get back as soon as I meet with President Redman again and have a green light.

Next I write a short prospectus of what I have in mind and submit it to President Redman. She calls me in, tells me she's studied it carefully, that it looks good, and to get started. She agrees with beginning modestly, and then, over time, augmenting the curricula and staff.

When I call Joyce Bennett to let her know it's a go, she says that she and her husband should be able to pack up and make the trip within a week or two. That's good news because the autumn semester is scheduled to begin in less than two months and we need to get together and work out all the details. She sounds enthusiastic, and I figure her for a good fit.

Ten days later, lugging a U-Haul, they arrive and find an apartment near the University. Her husband, Dave, is a journalist and aspiring novelist. He applies for work at the local newspaper and, because he has good credentials from having been a reporter with two newspapers, is hired.

Joyce also taught classes while getting her doctorate, so she's a proven quantity. We soon decide on the three three-hour classes she initially will teach.

The University has a cadre of experienced secretaries. One's hired.

The new Department is assigned a suite of four rooms in a newly constructed building on campus, with Joyce and me each having a room, another for our secretary, and the fourth for files and miscellany. The building has classrooms, so we'll be teaching there as well. Two other small departments also are being housed in the building.

Joyce and Dave both are experienced backpackers and wilderness buffs, as well as being trail-bikers, so it isn't long before they join Leah and me and the twin's en-route up the side canyon to the old house. Rather than walking, we take their advice and equip the family with trail-bikes, and that henceforth becomes our means of transportation. Great exercise for the legs, much faster than walking, and the twins are delighted.

Joyce and Dave both have fly fished for trout, but neither for steelhead, or have they ever sluiced for gold, so there's a lot to learn. It doesn't take them long to catch on. During three days each catches a steelhead and they are successful enough sluicing to pay for their first month's rent. While Dave and I bag grouse and Leah and Joyce collect chanterelles, the twins supply us with trout. As well as listening to the ubiquitous coyotes, one night we hear the plaintive howling of wolves. We also find the unmistakable imprints of a grizzly in mud along the stream.

"Pete, I now know why you turned down that cushy teaching position at the University."

"Yes, Joyce, we're really addicted to this little corner of paradise which we affectionately refer to as our North Cascades Shangri-La."

While there, Leah and I regale them with all our adventures and misadventures over the years in the side canyon and at the old homestead.

"All of this has been very interesting," Dave declares, "lots of great material for novels I have yet to write."

# *Chapter Nineteen*

Joyce and I are comfortable with the classes we've decided upon for the autumn semester. Because time is short, we're forced to rely mostly on what each of us already is prepared to offer. But it's important that we soon get a handle on our department's long term goals, so as we get ready to begin teaching, it's with that in mind.

My training and experience mainly has been with environmental politics, Joyce's with the scientific aspects of the environment. Her doctoral dissertation evaluated the effects clear-cutting of forests has on biodiversity. As such, our experiences complement each other.

We agree that because, initially at least, most of our students likely will be enrolled in other departments and be graduating as teachers, engineers, foresters, businessmen, and ranchers, our focus should be in familiarizing them with the basic environmental concerns they'll be dealing with as they go their various ways after graduation. And, because most are from within the Northwest and will be returning to their Northwest roots after graduation, our teaching mainly should concentrate on Northwest environmental issues.

Eventually, we foresee that more of our students than initially will be seeking degrees in Environment, but not for some years. However, we may be surprised and find it happening sooner because the environment has become such an important topic.

When registration is completed, we learn that as expected most of our students are majoring in other disciplines, but way more than we'd anticipated want an Environment major.

President Redman, learning this, asks Joyce and me to meet with her for an evaluation. She agrees that for the present we should continue as planned, but authorizes us to recruit two additional teachers for the spring semester and to tailor the curricula to provide a four-year degree in Environment. She assigns additional office space and classrooms.

The Pacific Northwest is one of the planet's most favored regions, with thousands of miles of ruggedly beautiful coastline, towering mountain ranges, hundreds of mostly free flowing rivers home to trout, salmon and steelhead, and vast forested areas harboring deer, moose, caribou, black and grizzly bear, wolves, cougar, ospreys and bald eagles, and countless other interesting species.

The only down-side is the inevitability someday of major earthquakes and volcanic eruptions. They happened in the not too distant past, and are predicted again, sooner rather than later. Several major earthquake fault lines cross the region, and nearby mountains, including Baker and Rainier, are slumbering volcanoes.

However, those dangers aside, even with all its beneficence, the vast region has serious environmental problems, so Joyce and I focus our teaching on them. To name some:

- Hatcheries are producing millions of young fish that compete with native stream-bred fish for food and space, and threaten vital genetic integrity.

- Old growth forests throughout southeast Alaska, and most lowland forested areas in Washington, Oregon, and British Columbia, are being clear-cut at an alarming rate, with devastating effects on fish, wildlife, and the environment.

- Some of the Northwest's largest rivers and many smaller ones have dams that hinder or stop salmon and steelhead runs and result in thousands of miles of tributary streams above the dams being unavailable to migrating fish. Thousands of needed or poorly designed culverts add to the problem.

- Urban and industrial pollution is contaminating ocean areas adjoining such large Northwest cities as Seattle, Portland, Vancouver, and Victoria, and lumber mills alongside many rivers continue to spew out PCBs and other pollutants.

- Dozens of Atlantic salmon fish farms along Northwest coastal and inter-coastal waters are sources of serious disease and pollution and are imperiling native fish.
- A huge influx of people with upward mobility aspirations, drawn to the region by all its thriving businesses and attractive surroundings, is impacting the environment.
- Urban sprawl around greater Vancouver, Seattle, and Portland is preempting thousands of acres of once prime forest, range, and farm land, with huge losses of space for native plants and wildlife.
- Visitors from cruise ships and other means of mass transportation threaten to overwhelm the Northwest's scenic areas and impair the ability of residents to enjoy their natural heritage.
- An environmental concern of another sort is the re-population of the region's wild places with wolves and grizzlies and the threat they pose to livestock and game.

So our job is to make our students aware of these and other Northwest environmental issues, help them to understand them, inform them of the trade-offs, and teach them how best to cope with and manage them.

As classes begin, all are full, mainly with students from other departments who recognize the need to learn about the environment. A surprising number, however, are freshmen hoping eventually to earn a degree in Environment so they too, as with Joyce and me, may have a hand in protecting it?

As Joyce and I pool our thoughts about the Department's long term goals and how best to achieve them, we decide on how to expand our curricula and what we're looking for in additional teachers. We agree that the curricula should over time conform essentially to what's being taught at the University in Seattle and other such institutions having Environment majors, except be more regionally oriented. We also agree that our new teachers, as well as being professionally proficient, also should have practical field experience.

The first two we select meet these criteria. One is from the Environmental Protection Agency in British Columia, and the other from The Wilderness Society's Portland office. Both have the kind of field as well as teaching experience we want. And both are eager to come aboard after learning about our plans for the new Department and that the College is now a fully accredited University. President Redman endorses our ambitions and plans and meets with the two new teachers.

\*\*\*\*\*\*\*\*\*\*\*\*\*

Leah and I get with Byron Hicks at faculty functions and, weather permitting, for trail-bike treks to the old homestead. He's settled nicely into the teaching routine, is enchanted with the Northwest, and reassures Leah that he is busily casting about for a wife.

Tom Strike, now a successful, respected, and prosperous Bellingham attorney and pal, has married Sally, the middle-school teacher Leah arranged for him to meet. She enjoys sluicing, they sometimes join us at the old house, and we regularly see them socially in Bellingham.

A pack of wolves definitely has taken up residence in the vicinity of the old homestead and, to our delight, occasionally are seen or heard. The only complaints are from hunters who half-facetiously claim the wolves are decimating the deer and elk herds. On one occasion we glimpse a grizzly, and sometimes find tracks. Each species, so far, has stayed out of trouble. Both are protected under the Endangered Species Act.

The twins now are in high school, and Leah

continues happily busy as a mom and matron. She's also president of the Faculty Club. My increased salary is appreciated because a year from now the twins leave for college. We still have some lode-claim money and all our Microsoft stock. Predictably, it's stopped splitting, but we can't complain. The 860 original shares are now almost 26,000.

# Chapter Twenty

Joyce and Dave have been in Bellingham several years and I had assumed all was well with them. Then, Joyce mentions that Dave has become frustrated with his work as a reporter. "He complains that the newspaper lacks the wherewithal and incentive to do much investigative reporting, and that's what he's experienced and best at and wants to do more of." She's concerned because he's become so discouraged.

I find this very troubling and join with her in trying to figure what to do. Finally, it occurs to me that the various Northwest environmental issues our classes are studying could use a lot more outside exposure and publicity.

"Joyce, do you think Dave's newspaper would be interested in doing a series of articles on Northwest environmental issues, the kind we're covering in our classes, and assign Dave to do the investigative reporting and writing?"

Her eyes light up, "Pete, that's exactly the sort of thing Dave would love to do. I'll see what he thinks and whether he believes the newspaper would be interested and assign him the work.

"Not only would it be great for Dave, but it would

juice up our classes. Our students could even pitch in and help. Think of all the practical experience they'd get."

So, she asks Dave, and he's immediately enthused. He discusses it with his editor and he thinks it a great idea. Both go to the publisher and he also likes it, except he says the paper can't cover the additional costs.

When Dave tells us what the publisher said, Joyce and I agree that it's too good an idea to let die, and then she remembers something she'd learned about President Redman.

"Pete, rumor has it that President Redman has tie-ins with some high-tech millionaires in Seattle. Why don't we see if she would be willing to ask them to ante up the money? I hear many have an environmental bent and are looking for positive ways to use their gains."

We arrange a meeting with the President.

"I'm intrigued with the idea and I just may know a few well-healed movers and shakers who would jump at the chance. I'll check with them, and then we'll go from there."

A week later she tells us, "There definitely is interest, but my contacts want to know more about what you have in mind. Give me something in writing that identifies the problems and details, including the kind of money the newspaper needs."

The three of us get together and within a week have fleshed out a proposal. We identify five critical environmental problems urgently affecting the Northwest. They are Asian drift net fishing, old growth clear-cutting, sea lion predation of salmon and steelhead, Atlantic salmon coastal and inter-coastal farming, and the effects of the Babine Lake sockeye hatchery on Skeena River steelhead.

We know that there's abundant information about each, but it will take a lot of work to pull the information together, update it, and frame in ways that make it meaningful. We can provide Dave a head start by making available everything we have in our files and are using in our classes, plus arranging for help from our students.

After consulting with his editor and publisher, Dave says they like the subject matter and figure about two years would be required to do a first class job of preparing and running a series of articles on the five problems. A million dollars should do it.

A week after we give our proposal to President Redman, she asks to meet again. "I have firm commitments for the $1 million, and as far as I'm concerned it's a definite go. I think the whole thing is a wonderful idea, both for the newspaper and for the

University and your students, and I can't wait to see the first series."

The three of us decide that the Asian drift net problem is the most urgent so, with the concurrence of his bosses at the newspaper, that's where Dave begins.

For years, Japanese, Taiwanese, and South Korean fishermen have been illegally catching large numbers of salmon and steelhead in immense North Pacific drift-net operations. The fishery ostensibly is to net squid, but the real objective is salmon. Huge numbers of salmon collect in the North Pacific prior to returning to rivers to spawn. Numerous boats, many deploying nets miles long and 35 feet deep, are believed to be harvesting a quarter or more of the salmon, plus many steelhead. In addition, many other fish and other sea life, including dolphin, whale, and other marine mammals, as well as sea birds, are indiscriminately being swept up and killed. The drift-nets are having a huge impact regionally because many of the salmon and steelhead being taken are bound for Northwest rivers.

Pressure is being applied by Russia, Canada, and the United States to get the culpable nations to stop, and a resolution banning their use is under active consideration before the United Nations. But it has yet to be adopted. The kind of publicity Dave's articles could generate may be critical.

Dave gets to work with the information we provide plus more he's able to gather from other sources. With help from our students, he prepares a comprehensive series of articles that reveal which nations are involved, how the boats operate, how long it's been going on, and the horrible consequences not only to salmon and steelhead but all other marine life in the North Pacific. Two months after Dave begins, the newspaper carries the series.

*Outrage* at what the series reveal is palpable throughout the Northwest because the drift-net operations had received so little attention. It's a revelation for thousands of readers. The articles are picked up by wire services and run in many other newspapers, not only in the Northwest, but throughout the US, Canada, and other nations riming the North Pacific, including the offending ones. Radio and TV outlets feature the articles. Pressure mounts in the United Nations to pass the resolution, and it soon is.

President Redman and the people she's enlisted are delighted and proud, as are our students, many of whom helped Dave.

With success of the drift-net series, and with four other series yet to be written, Dave has a new purpose in life.   Joyce tells me she can't believe the difference it makes in his attitude and outlook.  Even the newspaper, Dave says, has a whole new dynamic.

The three of us decide that the next series will be about the ongoing massive clear-cutting and impending loss of almost all of the Northwest's old growth forests, and the destructive environmental consequences, particularly on rivers and fish.

We've been hearing about the disappearance of endangered spotted owls as old growth stands continue being clear-cut.  So we decide to take a look ourselves. We hire a small airplane and as the three of us fly over Vancouver Island and the forests of Washington and Oregon, it's obvious that the logging industry is grossly abusing the intent.

About 90 percent of the magnificent old growth stands already are gone, and most of the lands where they stood have been converted into tree farms. *At stake is the remaining 10 percent.* There's no question that logging should and shall continue to be a major component of Northwest economic life, but not at the expense of the few remaining old-growth stands.

The type of logging we observe from the air has much broader implications than the loss of the remaining old growth stands.   Forested watersheds have the capacity to absorb and slowly disperse precipitation throughout the year. With good forest cover, stream flows and water temperatures fluctuate only moderately, regardless of the amount of precipitation. When watersheds are extensively and poorly logged, rivers massively flood and water temperatures wildly fluctuate. At risk are many if not most of the region's native salmon and steelhead runs.

Again, there's a wealth of information, including photographs, for Dave to draw upon. He need only tell the story so that it's accurate and intelligible to readers. However, because the series will blow the whistle on the forest industry, including the numerous involved federal and state agencies and private logging operations, the series is certain to be controversial, especially in the Northwest where logging still rules.

Dave meets with all the various interests, including both those whose livelihoods depend on logging, and those who want it scaled down. After several months he's hammered out an excellent series of articles that discuss all aspects of the problem and present an approach that allows sensible logging to continue, while preserving the remaining old growth stands.

Because the subject is so contentious, before the

series is released, Dave has President Redman and her cohorts in Seattle review the articles. They suggest a number of tactful changes.

As with the first series, it's reported in newspapers and other media outlets throughout the Northwest, and given extensive coverage in the US and Canada.

Dave, with student help, then prepares series on each of the other three problems we've selected. They, too, are featured in the newspaper and given extensive media coverage.

California sea lions pose a serious and ongoing threat to depleted salmon and steelhead runs. The Marine Mammal Act, passed in 1976 to mainly protect whales, polar bear, and sea otter, unwisely was broadened to include all marine mammals. The result, sea-lion numbers ballooned from less than 30,000 when the act was passed, to well over 100,000. With few natural predators, increasing numbers congregate at river mouths all the way from Southern California to the northern end of Vancouver Island mid-September through April, where they devour vulnerable fish entering their natal rivers.

In one example, sea-lions collecting at the mouth of the Ballard Locks leading into Lake Washington and its headwaters virtually eliminated a robust run of native steelhead.   Fish runs all along the Pacific Coast are similarly depressed and sea-lions are a major reason.

Atlantic salmon fish farms, proliferating within the coastal and inter-coastal waterways of Washington and British Columbia, especially the latter, pose another serious threat to native salmon and steelhead. The immense concentrations of penned-up salmon, located athwart native fish spawning routes, have become major sources of deadly disease and pollution.  Some Atlantic salmon also are escaping the pens and establishing runs of their own in direct competition with native fish.

The Skeena River in northern British Columbia and such renowned tributaries as the Copper, Babine, Kispiox, Bulkley, Sustut, and Morice, once teemed with magnificent races of native steelhead.  Then, in 1983, a huge hatchery at the head of the Babine River came on-line for the purpose of beefing up sockeye salmon numbers.

Adult sockeye,  returning to the Skeena  two or three years after being released as smolts from the hatchery, are eagerly sought by hundreds of  commercial fishermen who deploy  gill-nets  near the Skeena's mouth.  The problem is that because adult steelhead are similar in size to the sockeye, return at the same time, and co-mingle with them, huge numbers of steelhead (in some years 85 percent), are also being lost to nets. What once had been world class steelhead fishing in the Skeena and its tributaries is becoming little more than a memory.

The newspaper and Dave each receive a Pulitzer Prize for the five series of articles, their first.

With the success of the five series comes interest and financing for more of the same kind of articles.

One that we identify is that there is a marked disparity in appearance between the farms and rural areas in Washington, as compared with those in British Columbia. In Washington the rural landscape is cluttered with old abandoned rusting cars and farm machinery and other unsightly debris, while rural British Columbia mostly is uncluttered and neat.

Another is the widespread and indiscriminate dumping of trash, including such bulky items as old refrigerators, tires, and furniture, along remote side roads and out-of-the-way forested corners by residents too lazy and irresponsible to dispose of them properly.

Another is that market hunting and fishing is rampant in the Northwest, whereby game animals and fish are being illegally killed for under the counter sale. In Washington alone many hundreds of deer and elk are being slaughtered. Bear and other game animals are similarly being killed and body parts such as livers sold, mostly abroad. The practice extends even to oysters and other bivalves. In addition, many native plants illegally are being taken and sold for decorating.

Yet another is that poaching by disreputable individuals who disregard regulations designed to limit the taking of fish and game for the purpose of protecting the supply and assuring sufficient numbers survive to replenish the species, is a serious ongoing problem.

The long range solution for these and other such vexing problems is for schools to focus on them in their classes so that children are made aware of all that's at stake at an early age and throughout their schooling. Dave's articles strongly encourage the *school solution*, but stress that in the meantime state and local jurisdictions and the public-at-large can and should be doing much more.

As new problems arise or old ones call for more exposure, the newspaper and Dave do their duty, as do our students. The experience and training our students receive is invaluable and influences what many will do after they graduate.

All involved in the newspaper's and Dave's efforts continue being immensely pleased with what's being achieved. It's become one of those cooperative endeavors in which everyone who participates, benefits.

With expanding curricula and staff, the Environment Department is awarding four-year degrees, and the Department has taken its place alongside the University's other major departments.

In addition to my continuing responsibilities as a department Dean, President Redman selects me as a *Provost* to assist her in administering the University.

# Chapter Twenty-One

My father and I were very close and spent countless days fishing together throughout the Northwest. During those trips he delighted in reliving for me his many and varied outdoor experiences and adventures. Some of the most memorable happened during the two summers he served as a young fire-guard in Yellowstone National Park immediately following World War Two. One was in the Thorofare District which encompasses the park's southeast quarter, and the other in the Bechler District encompassing the park's southwest quarter. In addition to telling me about those two summers, Dad also wrote about them in a journal that I inherited.

The twins are fascinated with all I've told them about their colorful grandfather and what they've read in his journal, particularly his experiences in Yellowstone's Thorofare and Bechler districts, and anxiously have been planning to visit the two districts as soon as they graduate from high school, which just happened.

*In the balance of this chapter, Einar describes their week in Thorofare. He also relates some of their grandfather's experiences fifty years earlier. In the next chapter, Bruce does the same for their week in Bechler.*

In laying our plans for visiting Thorofare and Bechler, Bruce and I decide to be in Thorofare the last week in August and Bechler the first week in September. Any earlier and we risked encountering the intolerable swarms of mosquitoes and horseflies Granddad wrote about in his journal. They ceased being a problem with the first frost, about mid-August. So, by auto from Bellingham, we're finally on our way.

Granddad's initial duty as a fire-guard in Yellowstone was during the summer of 1946. He and about a dozen other aspiring young fire-guards spent their first week at park headquarters in Mammoth Hot Springs, where they were trained in their duties by assistant chief ranger Scotty Chapman. Scotty made an impression because he was freshly back from soldiering the past several years in the South Pacific and, due to all the quinine he'd been taking to ward off malaria, he had lost most of his hair and his skin was distinctly yellow. Following the week of training, the fire-guards were dispersed as two man teams to various locations throughout the park.

Fire-guards served primarily to suppress forest fires. When not fighting fires, they cleared fallen trees from park trails, re-hung telephone lines connecting the various ranger stations and patrol cabins, and carried-out various other backwoods tasks. Horses were assigned to pack their equipment.

Having been posted to the Thorofare District, Granddad, his partner, and their five horses, made their way by trail south along the east side of Yellowstone Lake to the Trail Creek patrol cabin at the lake's Southeast Arm, their base for the summer. Although in telephone contact at times with Bill Nyquist, their supervising district ranger, who was stationed at the Lake Ranger Station thirty miles north, the team essentially was on its own.

Granddad described one amusing incident that happened while they were at the Trail Creek patrol cabin. Anglers frequently motor-boated down the southeast arm because fishing for the 18 to 20 inch cutthroat trout was so good. One group, after catching several dozen and docking overnight at the patrol cabin, hung their catch on a cord they suspended between two trees, and then slept beneath on the ground. When they awoke next morning all that remained of all their fish were a few scraps. A bear had crept in, pulled the cord down, and consumed every last fish, all without awakening any of them. Tongue-in-cheek, Granddad wrote that he followed tracks left in sand by the bear, and found them deeper going than coming.

The upper Yellowstone River, southward from where it enters the Southeast Arm near the Trail Creek patrol cabin, was prime moose habitat. While working trail along the river, Granddad and his partner often picketed their horses overnight in nearby meadows. Usually, he wrote, when they retrieved the horses in the morning, they found them companionably sharing the meadows with a moose or two.

Once, in following a strand of the telephone line that had been dragged back into the woods, Granddad found the skeletal remains of a huge bull moose, its massive antlers entwined in the metal line. Seeing the way the line was twisted and knotted about the antlers and body, it wasn't difficult, he wrote, to imagine the desperate victim's drawn out yet futile struggle to escape.

Frequently at night, while sleeping on the ground, large animals, likely deer or elk, but possibly moose, tramped by, sometimes almost on top of them. Daunting at first, it soon became routine.

Although Granddad never came face to face with a grizzly that summer, he wrote that their signs were everywhere. The team spent some nights in patrol cabins. Invariably, the exteriors were scarred where grizzlies had attempted to tear their way in. "Oh, what a mess," the ranger told them, "when one succeeded."

He wrote that because the mosquitoes and horseflies were so bad, that it was possible to make a single swipe along the side of a horse and come away with a handful of insects.

Granddad's partner happened to be accident prone. Once, while the two were atop adjoining telephone poles re-hanging a section of line that had pulled loose, Granddad heard his partner cry out. Looking over, he saw that the pole his partner was on had broken off at the base and was falling. Contrary to what they had been warned, his partner had neglected to check whether the base was rotten. Luckily, his partner somehow managed to swing sideways before the pole hit the ground and avoided being crushed.

On another occasion near the end of the summer, one of their horses, an exceptionally large one named Duke, stomped down on his partner's foot, breaking a bone. This necessitated his being taken by boat back to the Lake Ranger Station for treatment, leaving Granddad to complete the summer alone, including having to *trail* the five horses single-handed back to the Lake Ranger Station.

Bruce and I decide that rather than reaching Thorofare by hiking or canoeing south through the park, we'll get there by backpacking north through the Bridger-Teton National Forest. Each of us is six foot, 170 pounds, and in excellent condition from having led a clean life, being active in high school athletics, and inheriting the right genes, so 60 pound packs aren't a problem.

After a long trek, we arrive at the Forest Service's Hawk's Rest patrol cabin, two miles south of the park, pitch our tents, and prepare to spend the night. Thankfully, no mosquitoes or horseflies.

Most of what we'll be eating in the coming days is freeze-dried, but we've planned something special this evening. First, potatoes are wrapped in aluminum foil and buried in campfire coals. An hour later, large juicy T-bone steaks are grilled over the fire. When the steaks are just the way we want them, the potatoes are raked out, and dinner is served.

Early next morning, we're off to the park. Our packs, in addition to tents, sleeping gear, and extra clothes, have maps, cameras, rain gear, an ax and saw, sandals for use in crossing streams, first aid kits, compasses, flashlights, binoculars, a cooking kit, fishing gear, bells to alert bears of our presence, and pepper spray to fend bears off.

The first place we head after crossing into the park is the historic Thorofare Ranger Station, a mile inside. One of first ranger stations built in Yellowstone, its main use now is by rangers who patrol the boundary during autumn elk hunts to make sure that hunters don't stray into the park

We pitch our tents near the station and for the rest of the day luxuriate in being at the heart of one of the country's largest and most remote wildernesses. Overlooking us east are the jagged Absaroka Mountains, and west the windswept Two Ocean Plateau along which follows the Continental Divide. Spread out before us in between is the broad valley of the upper Yellowstone River, interspersed with sagebrush flats, grasslands, marshy bogs, willow thickets, and groves of aspen and conifers. The river, after descending from its origins outside the park in Wyoming, wends north within the park for fifteen miles and enters Yellowstone Lake's Southeast Arm.

Thorofare is home to healthy numbers of moose, elk, mule deer, antelope, black and grizzly bear, and, in the craggy Absarokas, goats and sheep. Coyotes, wolverine, fox, and lesser carnivores, as well as Sandhill cranes, eagles, marsh hawks, and osprey also are relatively abundant. Game trails lace the valley floor. The only access is by boat down the lake's Southeast Arm, or by long distance trail.

Among Granddad's most stirring memories were his evenings in camp. He wrote:

"After a hard day clearing trail and hanging line, we'd find a good place to camp, build a fire, and have a hearty if not very tasty meal of bread, meat, potatoes, and vegetables, all from cans. Then, relaxing alongside the fire, I'd load the old *hod* and, puffing away, enjoy its companionship. The crisp night air was made all the more fragrant by the mix of pipe tobacco and campfire smoke. Later, after checking to make sure the horses hadn't tangled their picket lines, we'd place a few slow burning logs on the fire, and settle into our bedrolls. At odd hours, chipmunks scampering across our covers, sprinkles of wind-borne rain, or the footfalls of some nearby large animal, often caused a stir. Those evenings in that remnant of the old west gave lasting memories. The nostalgia remained after all else had faded."

Granddad described how once, as the two of them were crossing the valley with their pack-string of five horses, "A small low flying black and yellow plane belonging to some wealthy product of civilization crossed overhead. The pilot, observing our slow progress, probably sensed a ghost of the past, just as we seemingly part of that past, realized the incongruity of his presence."

In Granddad's day, a network of tiny patrol cabins spaced one day's snowshoe travel apart because they often were used in winter, served as convenient stopping points for rangers and fire-guards. Known as *snowshoe cabins*, they were joined by telephone lines and stocked with food, bedding, and firewood. Some still are in use, although radios have long since replaced telephones, and all the wire telephone lines have been removed.

Bruce and I plan to spend two days hiking north by trail along the river until we reach the Southeast Arm. We'll then retrace our steps, make a short side trip to tiny Bridger Lake that Granddad had written held large cutthroat trout, and finally return to where our auto is parked. This late in the year, at an elevation of 8,000 feet, the weather may quickly turn wintery, so we may have to leave in a hurry.

Underway, we're aware of the possibility of meeting up with grizzlies. To forestall encounters, we're alert so as not to surprise one up close, and have tied bells on our packs to warn of our presence. We've also made sure pepper spray is handy. That the schools of cutthroat trout moving out of Yellowstone Lake to spawn in the river already have come and gone, reduces the chance of bear.

Granddad wrote that the river holds large cutthroats. The first place we fish is alongside a wide sweeping hole made to order for such fish. I try a muddler, but it's ignored.

Bruce, fishing below, sees a hatch of Mayflies and ties on an imitation. Observing occasional swirls of fish after the Mayflies, he aims his fly near one and is immediately into a fish. It streaks strongly away and takes most of his line, only to throw the hook.

"Wow, that was one of the big ones," he shouts.

The next hour we catch half a dozen fish, but none over about 17 inches. Remembering Bruce's big one, as we continue down the trail, we keep trying.

Soon, we come to a small side-stream descending from the Absarokas. It looks to have fish, so we stop for a try, heading in opposite directions. If any are caught, we decide to keep two for dinner. I soon get a 13 incher, and Bruce calls that he's caught one too.

Then, concealed by an overhanging bush next the stream, something artificial catches my eye. Pulling the bush aside, I find a canvass-covering and beneath a gold-sluice similar to the ones we've been using in the side canyon. Knowing that sluicing is banned in the park, I look about for the owner and seeing no one, replace the cover, and go the find Bruce. I also mark its location on my map.

When Bruce learns of the sluice, he cautions, "Lets leave; we don't want to risk a run-in with whoever owns it." Still seeing no one, we continue down the trail.

A little later we stop again to fish. This time it's my turn with a big fish. Tying on a fly resembling one of the abundant grasshoppers, I float it down next to the undercut bank. Suddenly, a gaping mouth engulfs it. The fish shoots away and never stops until, noticing my line's almost gone, I tighten up and the leader snaps.

At least we know there still are hefty fish. Our problem may be that they're too hefty.

Several hours later and with evening at hand, we come to a grassy meadow that has a tree for hanging food, a nearby spring, and no visible grizzly tracks. Perfect for camping. Old fire-rings indicate others had the same idea. Across the river, a cow moose and twin calves, standing among willows along the edge, watch us.

From reading Granddad's account about the flu-like *Yellowstonites* park waters infamously cause, we're careful to treat our water. He wrote of never being sicker than the one time it laid him low. Perhaps the little spring *is* safe, but we don't take a chance.

The next morning we're on our way again, fishing some but mainly enjoying the scenery and watching and taking pictures of the various wild creatures of which one or more are almost constantly in view. A grizzly makes a brief appearance across the river, but disappears as soon as it whiffs us.

Toward evening, we arrive near where the river enters the lake. Because the area is so convoluted and marshy, we're unable to get close, so we make camp on an overlooking bluff. Spread out before us is the huge delta formed where the river enters the lake. Granddad wrote that the delta and surrounding marshes were a veritable wildlife bonanza. It's easy to see what he meant---moose are never out of sight

Early the next morning we begin retracing our steps and within a day and a half are again back at the ranger station. In route, we pause at several places to fish, but only catch more 15-17 inchers. That evening, sitting beside our campfire and enchanted by the wondrous scenery and the spell of undefiled wilderness, we're reminded what Granddad was thinking when he wrote, *'the nostalgia remained after all else had faded'*.

Our next objective is Bridger Lake, named after the famous mountain-man, trapper, and explorer. It lies a mile south of the park within the national forest. According to Granddad, "The little lake is a favorite stopping place for pack strings of tourists because of the abundant large cutthroat trout that thrive on swarms of tiny fresh water shrimp, fish up to five pounds or more."

To reach the lake, we begin by following a trail leading west from the ranger station for a mile along the park's southern boundary to an abandoned snowshoe cabin. Arriving, we find that the cabin's crumbling logs still bear evidence of grizzly tooth and claw marks. From there, a side trail veers south to Bridger Lake.

We're favored by continued good weather, and have the lake to ourselves. Abundant signs indicate that it's still a popular stopping place for pack strings. Along the shore, we climb aboard a rickety log raft with paddles, and work our way over near to where dimples of rising fish are seen. Soon, we're catching them, but instead of the hoped for five pounders, they're only tiny four or five inchers. Later, we learn that Bridger Lake still has lunkers, but one needs to wait until evening and then cast large black leach-like flies and work them deep.

Returning to shore, we follow a trail back to Hawk's Rest, and eventually south to our auto. Thus ends a week that met all our Thorofare expectations. As well as the amazingly varied and abundant wildlife, for us the special appeal was the sense that what we saw, heard, and experienced were essentially what Granddad had rhapsodized about and what the early Indians, trappers, and explorers must have known.

We're determined some day to return. Beckoning are hikes into the Absarokas and onto the Two Ocean Plateau. Also, a trail west to Heart Lake and Lewis Lake, and another north along the east side of Yellowstone Lake to Fishing Bridge.

Our next destination is Bechler. In route we stop at Yellowstone's South Entrance ranger station to report the gold-sluice and pinpoint its location. Several weeks after returning home, a letter arrives from the park superintendent thanking us for letting them know about the sluice. They'd suspected that sort of activity, but learning where it actually was happening enabled them to apprehend the culprit.

# Chapter Twenty-Two

*In this chapter, Bruce tells about his and Einar's week in the Bechler District, together with some of their grandfather's poignant experiences fifty years before.*

It's early September and Einar and I have arrived by road at the Bechler Ranger Station, located in the extreme southwest corner of Yellowstone. Bechler, encompassing the park's southwest quarter, is dominated by the expansive Bechler Meadows and the lofty and remote Pitchstone and Madison Plateaus. Similar to Thorofare, it's yet another enormous wilderness, abounding in wildlife.

At eight thousand feet, once temperatures dip to freezing, mosquitoes and horseflies, at least as bad as at Thorofare according to Granddad, no longer are a problem.

We pay our respects to the ranger and explain that our reason for coming is because a half century earlier, in 1947, our Granddad had spent a summer as a fire-guard at the ranger station, and in reading his journal we were captivated with all he had written about his experiences that summer and by his description of Bechler's attractions.

The ranger generously spends an hour showing us around the ranger station, including the living quarters and barn, and describing the kinds of activities they now undertake. The station's physical layout and operations, he says, still are much as they were in Granddad's day. Two fire-guards still are assigned, and there still are fires to fight and trails to maintain. One change he mentions is that most of today's fire-guards are young women.

All the time we're with him, he's obviously intrigued in listening to what we're saying about what Granddad had included in his journal about the station and Bechler.

Granddad wrote that he and his partner occupied half the living quarters at the ranger station, while district ranger Walt Gammill and his wife and two small children occupied the other half.

The half occupied by the two fireguards included a wood stove, electric lights, a refrigerator, and a kitchen tap with only cold water. There was no indoor toilet or shower. Dirty clothes had to be hand washed on a scrubbed-board in water heated on the stove

Adjoining the living quarters was a large barn that included a work shop, hay loft, and stalls for the five horses. The horses carried the gear the two fire-guards used in fighting fires, clearing trails, and maintaining telephone lines. That particular summer, there were no fires.

About half their time was spent away from the station clearing trails and hanging lines. When at the station, they had various tasks to perform. One was climbing by ladder to the top of a tall lookout tower located nearby, and scanning the surrounding countryside for signs of smoke.

Another, each morning and evening, was monitoring the station's weather station and recording temperature, humidity, and wind direction and speed.

Yet another was felling dead trees in nearby woods and then bucking them up into firewood for use at the station. Since chain saws weren't permitted, the work was all accomplished using long two-man saws and double-bit axes. The two became adept at sharpening the saws and axes they used in supplying the station with firewood and in clearing fallen trees from trails.

Walt Gammill also had them drive the station pickup to Ashton, Idaho, 20 miles away, for food and other supplies.

Although Granddad never actually saw a grizzly while at Bechler, he often sensed their presence and found tracks and logs they'd ripped apart looking for ants and grubs. However, in between when he and his partner completed their week of training at Mammoth, and when they arrived to begin their summer at Bechler, they had a close call with a grizzly.

The two happened to be clearing trail back of the Lake Ranger Station on the west side of Yellowstone Lake. For some time elk had been heard milling about out of sight ahead in the woods up ahead. Suddenly, about a dozen cows with calves came dashing out of the woods in their direction. Right behind was a large grizzly hoping to catch one of the calves. The two fire-guards immediately climbed trees. No sooner were they safely out-of-reach, than the animals arrived beneath and stopped.

Next, one of the little calves, straying away from its mother, wandered near the bear, which immediately began chasing it. Just as the bear was closing in, the calf tripped and fell down. Granddad figured that was the end of the calf. However, before the bear could grab it, the calf jumped up and darted off to the side. Unable to turn quick enough, the bear was foiled, and the calf escaped back to its mother.

After about ten minutes, the whole group began moving away. A little later, when none were visible or could be heard, the two fire-guards climbed down and warily made their way back to the ranger station, careful to be near climbable trees as they went.

Shortly after Granddad and his partner arrived at Bechler, Walt Gammill took them on a long horseback trip lasting several days to familiarize them with the district. One of their nights was spent in the Buffalo Lake snowshoe cabin, high atop the remote Madison Plateau. In hopes of seeing a grizzly, Granddad arose just as it was getting light and stole to the shores of the lake. He missed *seeing* a grizzly, but not by much; fresh tracks were found in the sand. Those tracks were all it took to make the occasion unforgettable.

Moose were abundant in and about the Bechler Meadows. One cow and calf in particular frequented a section of trail Granddad often took to reach a particular stream to fish. The first time or two he encountered them the cow appeared uneasy and even menacing, but she soon decided he wasn't a threat, and thereafter whenever they met he was virtually ignored.

Crossing the vast Bechler Meadows was one of the fire-guards more challenging undertakings. The Meadows were home to a particularly savage species of horsefly that viciously attacked anything that left the forest. Whenever the fire-guards and their horses crossed the Meadows, the horses, knowing what awaited them, uncontrollably would begin running and wouldn't stop until the far side several miles away was reached and they once were again beneath trees and free of horseflies. The *challenge* was in making sure ahead of time the packs were securely tied down. If not, as the horses wildly ran, the packs inevitably worked loose and either cartwheel off or spilled their contents.

In talking with the ranger the first day, Einar and I described one trail in particular that Granddad had taken that resulted in an unforgettable experience. The trail, he wrote, headed north from the ranger station and after several miles crossed a tiny stream that held Brook trout. Not being native to the West, those Brook trout were the results of *plantings* someone had made. The ranger believes he knows the trail, and points out where it begins.

So that's where we head the next morning with a lunch and our fishing rods. After about three miles, the trail intersects a trickle of water. Following the trickle, we find a series of intermittent small pools, each with one or two plump beautifully colored Brook trout, to about ten inches. Several are caught and then carefully released. Almost certainly, these are descendents of the same fish Granddad experienced.

If he could have watched, it would have delighted him to see a repeat of his own indelible experience.

The following day Einar and I hoist our packs and head northerly from the ranger station along the main trail that leads first to the Bechler Meadows, and then up Bechler Canyon and onto the Pitchstone Plateau. We figure on spending as much as a week. The ranger warns us to be ready for a quick return if the weather changes.

The first three miles, all the way to the Meadows, are forested and relatively level. The Meadows appear almost limitless and dominate the landscape. Looking about, moose are visible at scattered points in the distance. About half way across the Meadows, we come to the Bechler River and soon find a good place to camp.

Granddad had written that the river offered excellent cutthroat fishing, including some over five pounds. Also, that large numbers of elk descended from their summer range atop of the high plateaus this time of year, with bugling by the rutting bulls a common sound.

We set up camp and then begin fishing. The secret he wrote was to float grasshoppers along the undercut banks where trout are poised to arch up and snatch them.

Grasshoppers are abundant, and it works. In the next few hours each of us catch half a dozen good-sized fish, up to about three pounds. One is kept for dinner.

After enjoying two exciting days of fishing and wildlife watching, we break camp and head for the

Bechler Canyon and then the Pitchstone Plateau, figuring to return for more of the same on the way back. Half a day later, we arrive where the canyon begins, and spend the night.

The Bechler River forms where three small rivers come together near the canyon's head atop the Pitchstone Plateau. The river then cascades for seven miles down the deep canyon before reaching the Meadows, its descent punctuated by a continuous series of waterfalls.

While clearing trail along the canyon floor next to the river, Granddad wrote how enraptured he was with the beauty of the waterfalls, some of Yellowstone's best. He also told of gorging on unbelievably abundant huckleberries. And, near where the three rivers come together, of finding a thermal area with a hot-spring that had just the right dimensions and water temperature for a refreshing sauna-like emersion.

Next morning, Einar and I begin the arduous seven mile tramp up the canyon. The topography quickly changes from being almost level and easy to being moderately steep and difficult. As we climb, it's just as Granddad told, a succession of beautiful waterfalls, one after another, all the way to the top, and bushes heavy with huckleberries.

Upon reaching the summit, with the Pitchstone

Plateau extending before us, we soon come to where the three rivers meet, and then to the thermal area and what has to be the same sauna-like hot-spring he described. No time's lost before we're relaxing in the pleasantly warm water.

According to Granddad, the river adjacent to the thermal area was loaded with *Rainbow* trout whose descendents had once been planted, because as with Brook trout, Rainbows aren't native to the region.

So we set up camp and begin casting. The Rainbows still are there, but in nothing like the numbers he described. Pack-strings, over the years, had taken their toll. Finally, two of about twelve inches are caught for supper.

We're careful to suspend our food from a tree and leave nothing lying about. The abundance of huckleberries undoubtedly means bear.

We remain two more days for more hot-spring use and fishing, but mainly to explore and see something of the remotely beautiful Pitchstone Plateau. Again, we're imbued with the same feelings as at Thorofare of being amidst an expansive wilderness.

As we descend Bechler Canyon, we find it's just as scenic as when we climbed up, but a lot easier. Midway we meet a pack-string with five tourists (*dudes* they're called in the park) and two wranglers on their way to the top, and eventually by trail all the way to Old Faithful.

Again reaching our camping spot along the Bechler River and with the weather still cooperating, we decide to remain two more days. The fish oblige, moose, deer, and Sandhill crane are frequently in view, elk bugle, coyotes serenade, and bear, undoubtedly present, leave us alone. What more could we wish?

As Einar and I say goodbye to the ranger and head back to Bellingham, it's with a grateful sense of wonder at all we've seen and done the past two weeks, first at Thorofare, and then at Bechler. How comforting to know that two such sublime preserves exist and, because of their location within Yellowstone, they'll still be here when we return.

# Chapter Twenty-Three

Einar and Bruce are away at college, and Leah and I have settled into the busy but pleasant existence we've come to associate with faculty life at a university.

Congressman Bob Dennis finally concludes he's had enough rough and tumble in the Nation's Capitol and has decided not to seek reelection. He's even given up running for the Senate. While flirting with the idea of trying for his House seat, Leah and I decide maybe someday, but not now.

I carry out my responsibilities as a department Dean and Provost, and I also continue to beat the drums about the two issues so important to me, that of saving the native salmon and steelhead runs and strengthening the Fish and Wildlife Department, even though I'm no longer a commissioner.

Several times I testify before the state legislature at Fish and Wildlife Department hearings, and it begins to appear in some respects that the situation is improving. The Department finally is focusing more on protecting native runs than turning out hatchery plants, and they've reined in some hatchery operations. Nevertheless, the numbers of native salmon and steelhead continue to decline. Some years are better than others, but the trend is steadily downward, at least within Washington.

Why? Because most native runs still are suffering the consequences of all the dams, bad logging, hatcheries, and other abuses they've been subjected to for so long.

Another reason is a quantum jump in the number of anglers.

Leah and I have resigned ourselves to catching only the occasional steelhead, instead of the dozen or so a year we once did. Rather than continuing to endure all the competition and lack of results, we've begun availing ourselves more of fishing opportunities at the various fly-in resorts and camps in the far-off areas of British Columbia and Alaska. Not as convenient and a lot more expensive, but wonderful sport.

During an early September trip to a fishing camp in Alaska's Bristol Bay region with Einar and Bruce along, the float plane shuttling us to the camp has engine trouble over a particularly isolated area and makes an emergency landing on a remote lake. After touching down, a gust of wind causes the plane to veer against the rocky shore. The plane remains upright and afloat, but is sufficiently damaged that it won't fly again without repairs.

To further complicate matters, the plane is lodged beneath a dense cover of overhanging trees that obscure it from being spotted from above. In addition, its radio has ceased operating, and the pilot had taken the GPS in for repairs and neglected to retrieve it.

While being shaken up, no one is injured. Fortunately, the plane is equipped with survival gear, including two large tents, sleeping bags, rain gear, and food.

The twins both are robust and athletic, Leah and I are similarly endowed, and all four are experienced campers. The pilot, while not a veteran Alaska bush pilot, has been piloting in Alaska long enough to be competent in this kind of emergency situation. He also is a former Navy Seal.

We clamber ashore carrying the survival gear and soon have a camp set up beneath the canopy of trees and close to the plane. Normally, it would only be a matter of radioing for help or relying on GPS to reveal our location, but with neither available we must devise other ways to help searchers find us.

Not a desperate situation, or is it? The weather is mild, but this late in the year it could turn cold with snow a possibility.

Duke, the pilot, assures us that when we don't

show up at the fishing camp, they'll report it by radio and an immediate search begin. He tells us he filed the mandatory flight plan, but then strayed off some distance because of wanting to check out some new unfamiliar country.

"So we may not see search planes right away. We have enough food to last a week if we take it easy, and there likely are fish in the lake."

When we get around to figuring out how best to help searchers, Duke says, "The plane unfortunately is hidden beneath trees, but its shiny surface may show through. Also, the plane is equipped with a large brightly colored raft that I'll inflate for shoving out from beneath the trees as soon as a search plane shows up."

"A third possibility is smoke from a fire, so we need to collect lots of dry wood," I offer.

"Why don't you boys hike over to that point and see if you can catch some fish," Leah suggests, pointing to a rocky shelf that juts into the lake about 75 yards away.

"Be on the alert for bear." Duke warns. "If you see one, hurry back to camp. If it comes at you, use this pepper sprayer," and hands a canister to each of them, "and remember you can't outrun a bear, they're too fast, so as a last resort curl up on your stomach and keep still."

The boys set up two spin-rods, get some red and white Daredevils, and head over to the point. Leah and I begin gathering wood for a fire. Duke goes to the plane, inflates the raft, and ties it alongside.

Duke also attempts to get his radio working. According to him, "It quit while we were still in the air, otherwise when I knew we were going down, I would have sent a *Mayday*."

The twins return after about an hour without having caught anything. "Once, something followed my spoon," Bruce says, "but it wouldn't take hold."

Night is near at hand, so Leah with help from Duke builds a small fire and heats some emergency rations for dinner. After eating, we retire to the tents, with the pilot and twins in one, and Leah and me in the other. When morning comes, there's a sheen of frost over everything.

I build a fire and begin heating water so we'll have something hot to drink with the breakfast Leah's preparing. As with last night's rations, the fare is Spartan, but loaded with calories and quite filling.

Duke then bundles all the food back inside the plane to lessen the chance of bear.

It's arranged that at least one of us is on the

lookout for rescue planes throughout the daylight hours. The boys return to the rocky point for more fishing and eventually catch two pike, each about five pounds. In cleaning them, they know to toss the entrails well out into the lake and wash the rocks clean of blood.

That's the pattern of our existence for the next two days. No search planes come and all we can do is stay alert and be ready to act quickly if we see or hear one.

About noon on the fourth day, the boys shout from the shelf where they're fishing, "We see a bear!"

Leah calls, "Come back to camp!"

"We can't, it's too close!"

Then, both boys dive in the lake, with a large bear right behind.

Duke immediately heads to the point with his pistol.

Helplessly, we watch as the bear catches up to one of the boys and grabs a leg. Then, we hear two shots and we see the bear veer away from the boys and head over toward where Duke's standing.

Both boys continue swimming and soon climb ashore at camp. Bruce is able to walk, but one pants leg is ripped, his calf is streaming blood, and the shoe is missing.

Duke takes another shot at the bear as it

approaches him, and then turns and begins running back to camp shouting for us to get into the plane, which the four of us quickly do.

By then, Duke arrives with the bear close behind and gaining. He turns, fires another shot, and then begins clambering into the plane with the bear having hold of a leg. I grab Duke and pull him inside, while he kicks free of the bear.

With Duke inside, Leah slams the hatch to prevent the bear from entering.

The bear at first stalks back and forth nearby, but then wanders off and soon is lost to sight. Possibly, it had been struck by several bullets and may have been mortally wounded, but the last we knew it was still functional and very belligerent.

Leah assesses Bruce and Duke's damaged legs. The bites are painful, but no arteries are pierced. After retrieving the plane's first aid kit, she cleans, disinfects, and bandages the wounds. With Duke instructing, she next administers painkillers and antibiotic shots. From his Navy Seal days, Duke's an expert in emergency first aid.

Handing me his pistol, Dukes directs, "Be alert. If the bear returns and tries to break into the plane, aim at its eyes and keep shooting."

The bear, still not visible, likely is nearby and eager for another chance at us.

"The bear's an old brownie, a boar," Duke says, "and because he's so emaciated I'd guess he's desperate for food. Usually, this late in the year, brownies are rolling in fat and headed for hibernation. Most, in this part of Alaska, aren't aggressive. Probably, he attacked because of hunger, as well as being old and cantankerous."

That he's hungry and old and cantankerous may explain his actions, but it doesn't alleviate our situation any. Here, the five of us are, crowded together inside a small plane, not knowing whether or when it will be safe to emerge. The hope is that the bear either has permanently vacated the area, or died from bullet wounds.

Because Duke earlier had moved all our food into the plane, food isn't an immediate worry. What does concern us is keeping warm if we have to remain in the plane, as all our sleeping bags and cold weather gear are outside at camp. Also, we must remain on the alert for searchers, and then catch their attention. It's important too that we get Duke's and Bruce's damaged legs to a doctor.

Several hours of daylight remain and we still

haven't eaten lunch, so Leah prepares a combination lunch-dinner. After an hour and still no bear, I say, "I'm going ashore to gather up our sleeping and cold weather gear and bring it inside."

Duke offers, "I'm mobile enough to go with you and fend off the bear if he shows up."

"Sounds good. Until we actually know the bear's left or dead, there's no way we can sleep ashore tonight or any night, simply too dangerous." Leah reasons.

"Here, take this pepper sprayer and I'll carry one too, as well as my pistol."

So, out of necessity, the two of us leave the plane and, with Duke watching for the bear, I hurriedly gather up our things in camp. We make it back okay, but without learning any more about the bear.

Following a cramped night in the plane, the five of us are greeted by another day of clear skies and renewed hope that rescuers soon may show.

After breakfast, Duke says, "I'm going to take the raft out to the middle of the lake in case someone flies over."

"How about me coming too?" Einar offers.

"Sure, there's room, and four eyes and ears are better than two. I'm also taking a mirror to reflect the sun if a plane appears."

"Also," advises Leah, "take some food and sun lotion."

"Here, Pete, I'll leave the pistol with you."

"Why don't you two go out for half the day, and then Leah, Bruce, and I'll relieve you for the other half," I suggest.

Duke, wistfully, "It's been four days since we crash landed. Figuring they'll keep broadening the search, there's a good chance we'll soon be found."

That afternoon, with Leah, Bruce, and me in the raft, Bruce hears a plane. Soon, Leah and I also hear it, and then it's seen approaching the lake. Leah's busy with the mirror as the plane passes overhead. It then begins circling down until it finally lands and taxis over next to us.

The pilot leans out and with a big grin, asks, *"Are you the missing Ecklands?"*

Obviously relieved and gratefully smiling back, we briefly tell him what happened and point to the downed plane over along the shore beneath the trees. At water level it's visible. "We'll meet you there," and begin paddling back.

The rescue plane isn't large enough to ferry all of us out in one trip, but after two flights everyone is safely back in Anchorage and Duke's and Bruce's legs have been examined and dressed. Some deep punctures, but nothing serious.

Later that month, we hear from Duke. "With some expert help, I was able to repair the plane and fly it off the lake. We found the bear about a hundred yards back of our camp, dead. Likely it died that first day, but there's no way of knowing. There were three bullet holes."

The fishing camp graciously informs us that we either may have back all we paid, or use it on a return trip next year. We choose the latter.

Duke probably saved Bruce's life when he ran over to the point and fired at the bear. We also are impressed by the way he handled the entire incident, but because he'd been a Navy Seal, it isn't a surprise.

The next year, upon returning to Alaska, we ask that he be the one to fly us to the fishing camp, but *only* if he remembers the GPS.

# BOOK THREE.  CULMINATION

## Chapter Twenty-Four

Two years later President Redman accepts the presidency of another university in eastern Washington. In leaving, she campaigns for me to replace her, the Board of Regents and Governor agree, and I'm named to the position.

My first act as University President is to appoint Joyce Bennett to succeed me as Dean of the Environmental Department.  We've served together for almost six years and jointly have shepherded the department until it's become one of the universities most respected.

My years as Dean and Provost, as well as my time with the congressman and as a Fish and Wildlife Commissioner, have provided me with the kind of experience and contacts one needs to be an effective President.  As such, the breadth of my duties range all the way from interviewing and recruiting faculty, to overseeing  the school's operations and management, to lining up and securing contributions from donors, to appearing before the state legislature to explain and justify budget requests, to charting the direction the University is heading.

Leah and I have moved into the President's residence. The twins, after being away at other universities, have graduated, both with law degrees, and returned to Bellingham to practice. Each is now married. While Leah and I occasionally visit favorite steelhead rivers, it's nothing like it once had been, and it appears the Fish and Wildlife Department may be running out of options.

This profoundly saddens me, as it does anyone who's ever known the ultimate in fishing experience that seeking and battling a steelhead provides. That the fish are no longer readily available to challenge anglers along all but a few of Washington's rivers is incomprehensible, yet it's happened.

Einar and Bruce, over the years, have returned several times to Yellowstone's remote Thorofare and Bechler districts and become well acquainted with all they have to offer. On one occasion, we accompany them and experience firsthand what my father once had known and what Einar and Bruce have come to cherish.

We return annually to Alaska for the wonderful fishing it offers. Duke, who spends winters in Yakima and summers in Alaska, regularly pilots us to the best spots.

Leah's parents, now quite elderly, have moved to Bellingham and are living near us in a senior community condo. They still are reasonably mobile, alert, and positive, and we often get with them. No more moose hunting for Bruce, but they relish the trout we give them, and the venison and occasional elk cuts as a result of our side canyon bow-hunting. They would like joining us at the old house but, not being trail bikers, the seven mile hike rules that out.

They knew when they decided to join us in Bellingham, that the move wouldn't be a hardship. The town is one of the Pacific Northwest's choicest places. It fronts on Puget Sound with the beautiful San Juan Islands only a short boat ride away, is only minutes from Mount Baker and less than an hour from the North Cascades, and is home to a medium sized university. The unsophisticated small town appeal that made it such a wholesome place to grow up in has been retained, even though it's now twelfth in size in the state with a population of 75,000. Its appeal is further enhanced by a pleasant ocean-front four season climate.

Today, Bob Dennis and Tom Strike, both now established and successful Bellingham attorneys, and Dave Bennett, Joyce's husband and a syndicated columnist, join me for lunch at the Faculty Club. For several years the four of us have been getting together two or three times a month. We find it stimulating to sit down with good friends over a meal and discuss hot-button topics covering a full range of state, national, and world issues, as well as to wrestle with myriad local and regional problems. Other townsfolk and visiting acquaintances sometimes join us.

One of the things the four of us have in common is a moderately-conservative political philosophy, and a serious concern that the state and country have for quite some time been headed in the wrong direction. President Clinton, at the goading of the Republicans, had ended Lyndon Johnson's welfare state and balanced the budget, so there had been hope. But, with 9/11, Al-Qaeda and Taliban terrorism, the wars in Afghanistan and Iraq, the Great Recession, a national debt of $15 trillion, annual trillion dollar budget deficits as far as the eye can see, and a seeming leadership vacuum in Washington DC, as well as a vastly changing world with an emerging China and India, the Muslim situation, and the world becoming overpopulated, from any point of view, the prospects are anything but rosy.

Of more immediate concern are the country's 10 percent unemployment and 20 percent underemployment, and the possibility that it may be sliding into another recession.

After orders are given for lunch, I lead off. "Well, where are we, gents? Anything good happening?"

"We were out in the Sound yesterday," Dave says, "and caught several nice silvers. The fishing's been good lately. Any of you want to try it, give us a ring. Our boat's just right for a day on the water. It's even got a cabin."

"I attended a meeting in Washington last week called by the President," Bob reports, "and sorry to say those back there don't yet have credible answers to any of the nation's many problems, including the really serious unemployment."

"What's needed," I say, "is for the country's small business people to get back again to making shoes and clothes and the million other things they once turned out before fair-trade and globalization."

"Yes," Tom adds, "most of those kinds of jobs have been exported to China, India, and the other emerging countries."

"So, how do we get them back?" Dave asks.

"For one, we need to fix the crummy tax system. Give the moms and pops some incentive to go back to work. The banks and the bureaucrats can fix this, if they'll just do it," Bob offers.

"Agree, for sure," I say, "we know the big boys are sitting on tons of capital that's just waiting there, hoping for a home. They could be lending that cash to the little guys, let them get back to work."

"You talk about any of that sort of thing in DC?" Tom asks.

"Nope, I heard nothing new and what I did hear had no zip to it. It's really discouraging. With some imagination and decent leadership, we could let the people with brains and initiative go at it, *entrepreneurs*, I believe they're called."

"Are there any Dick Cheneys around? We sure could use more like him."

"A few American companies *are* willing to make less, just to keep their people working." Tom offers, "One's the New Balance Shoe Company in Fallmouth, Mass. I use their jogging shoes and know something about them. What's needed is for more companies to take that sort of unselfish patriotic approach."

"Maybe," I add, "we could put the bite on our best and brightest right here in Washington. If they'd be willing to get out front on these things, a lot of others would follow."

During the discussion, lunch is served and we're

busy eating. We don't decide anything, but some fertile thoughts emerge.

The next day I ask Leah to invite Bob Dennis and his wife Marge over for dinner. I want to pick up on the ideas that came up at the lunch yesterday, and inject an idea or two of my own. I'm also hoping that Bob, armed with some fresh new ideas, decides to run for Governor. The present Governor has declared that she doesn't intend to seek reelection.

At dinner with Bob and Marge a few days later, the talk initially is mostly about the topics covered during the recent lunch.  Bob and I, following the lunch, each had briefed our spouses, so they're up-to-date.

Half way through the main course, I offer some of the ideas that had occurred to me since the lunch, and then begin steering the conversation to where I hope Bob will start thinking about running for Governor.

"I've given more thought to what we could do to alleviate unemployment, folks, and it seems to me that we have a unique opportunity right here in Washington to set an example for the rest of the country. We have some of the nation's most enterprising businessmen and successful companies.  Why don't we challenge the leaders of Amazon, Costco, Microsoft, and Starbucks, and, yes, Boeing, to bring back some of the jobs they've exported overseas? Sure, they'll have to give up some bottom-line profits, but it would be the patriotic thing to do, and it would give them excellent PR."

Then, as an example of what I have in mind for the state's mega-companies, I mention The New Balance Shoe Company Tom had cited at our recent lunch and its willingness to accept lower profits by continuing to produce its shoes in Massachusetts rather than exporting the work overseas.

Bob quips, "I sure think Boeing would react favorably, considering all the lost time and added expense it's incurring as they try farming out the building of Dreamliner components overseas."

Continuing, I say, "Another idea, I'd like to see a new stripe of candidate make a run for Governor, someone who's conservative in the sense of being in favor of private enterprise, small government, low taxes, and states' rights, but who also supports environmental protection. In other words, a *Green Conservative*. The state is ripe for serious change, just as the country is. If someone were to run on a conservative platform that pushes imaginative job creation, plus safeguarding the environment, I believe that person would win."

As if on cue, Leah suggests, "With a new Governor next year, it would be a natural for someone seeking the job to include what you two are talking about as a major part of his or her platform. If the idea were to take hold, it would almost guarantee election."

"I sure agree," Bob says. "There's no question that the people are ready for change. They're fed up with the business as usual mentality, whether in Washington DC or Olympia. I've even been giving some thought to making a run myself! What do you think of that?"

Leah and I, exchanging glances, both trumpet the idea. Marge, too, appears to be interested. From my own point of view, the main thing I'd hoped to achieve at dinner, just happened.

After dinner, as Bob and Marge are going out the front door, Bob turns and says, "We need to think a lot more about my running, but I'm beginning to like the idea. The prospects and timing are good. But it needs fleshing out. Bring it up at the next lunch, Pete, will you?"

# Chapter Twenty-Five

A few days later, Bob, Dave, Tom, and I meet again for lunch at the Faculty Club. Dave and I have invited our spouses as well, figuring the way our discussions are going that a woman's point of view is needed. Both Joyce and Leah are politically savvy and have strong feelings about the direction the state and country are headed and the urgent need to push for a change of course.

After everyone has arrived and ordered, I begin the discussion.

"You recall that when we met a week ago we agreed that there is an urgent need for change, both in Washington DC and in Olympia. We'll be choosing a new Governor next November and I believe someone with our political beliefs has a good chance of being elected, provided that person is able to put forth a persuasive program that results in lots of new jobs being created in the state.

"While at our house for dinner a few nights ago, Bob, here, told Leah and me that he's been giving some thought to making a run for Governor. If you all agree and are willing to help him put together a convincing platform to reverse the way the state's headed, I believe

Bob would be a most appealing candidate, a superior Governor, and would have an excellent chance of winning the election. What do the rest of you think?"

Dave Bennett is the first to voice an opinion. "Following our get together at lunch a week ago, I told Joyce what we had talked about and, having heard that the present Governor won't be seeking reelection, we began discussing who has our beliefs and would make a good candidate. Bob Dennis immediately came to mind, and, in fact, we were going to suggest it today, only Pete beat us to it."

"I can't agree more," Tom Strike says, "I believe we all favor the idea and it should only be a matter of getting it launched. I propose that, as of today, we comprise a committee for that purpose." Everyone agrees.

A beaming Bob Dennis has the next say. "Thanks, all, for your support. As I told Pete and Leah the other evening, the state needs serious change and I'd like to be the one to bring it about." And, with a chuckle, "All that's needed is a campaign fund of about $20 million, and the support of most the state's voters.

"Getting serious, the other evening Pete reminded me that the state is home to some the nation's most successful businessmen. They include the heads of such world class companies as Amazon, Costco, Microsoft, Starbucks, and Boeing. He believes that one way to create a lot of new jobs in the state would be to persuade them to bring back some of the work they've exported. Pete also believes it's time that we here in the Evergreen State begin aggressively emphasizing environmental protection. Carrying these ideas a step further, Pete suggested that rather than calling ourselves Democrats or Republicans, we adopt the label, *Green Conservative*. I like these ideas, endorse them, and believe that with them as the cornerstones of our platform, we would have a good chance of succeeding."

"I'm excited!" Joyce exclaims. "The state desperately needs imaginative changes in both its leadership and direction. I can't think of a better way to appeal to all those who'll be needed to achieve these changes than to adopt a catchy new label that puts a handle on what Bob wants to happen."

"How right, Joyce," Bob affirms. "What's needed next is a statewide announcement of my possible candidacy as a Green Conservative that spells out the goals that I would seek to achieve, explains the meaning of Green Conservative, and invites a show of support. Then, once we know the reaction, we can gauge whether my candidacy has wheels."

Dave responds, "Why don't I draft a media release for the consideration of everyone here today that covers what we're talking about? Once we all agree on the wording, I'll see that it's widely distributed. I can have a draft in your hands by tomorrow. Let me know how it can be improved, I'll make the changes, and have it ready for our next meeting."

"Moved and seconded."

Tom asserts, "I'll be particularly interested in the reaction of the big players at Microsoft, Amazon, Starbucks, Costco, and Boeing, because they're the ones Bob will be counting on to provide most of what will be needed to get him elected, specifically, moral support and money. And, after he's elected, step up and fulfill what he's promised, bring jobs back and create new ones."

"Yes, their acclaim and active support will be essential if Bob is to have any chance," Leah adds.

"*Green* may be a stumbling block," I put in, "Businesses are better known for discouraging environmental protection than they are of favoring it. Somehow, we need to convince those in the business sector that protecting the environment will result in added job creation and be in their best interests; also that it's *ethically* right."

"I'll see what I can do to frame the media release so that we dampen  that concern," Dave replies, "but  in a state  so generously endowed with  scenery and natural resources and so dependent upon all the tourism they generate, it makes sense that  the Green label  should resonate."

"If everyone agrees, we'll meet a week from now to consider Dave's media release.   Also, assuming the announcement's results are encouraging, it's not too early to begin thinking about the next steps we need to take to get Bob's campaign under way.  Any dissent?"  There is none.   "Then I'll see you all here in a week."

The next day, each of us gets a draft media release from Dave.  He receives a few suggestions,   revises the draft, and has it in our hands in time for the next lunch.

*Draft Media Release (as revised):*

*Former congressman Bob Dennis of Bellingham has announced that he may decide to enter the race to be Washington's next Governor.   "It's time for a change of direction in our state and I would like to be the one to bring it about.  I would challenge the state's world class businessmen and businesses to step up and create the new jobs we need to put thousands back to work.  If our unemployment crisis is to be solved, these CEOs and their companies are the ones best suited to get it done, not the bureaucrats in Olympia."*

*Bob Dennis is convinced that, with a strong show of patriotism, those businessmen and their companies, with their vaunted and proven ingenuity, can spur the start-up of many new small businesses that will bring back thousands of those high paying jobs that were shipped overseas.*

*He wouldn't run as a Democrat or Republican, but instead as a 'Green Conservative'. "It's time we get back to the Conservative principles that made our state so great, and it's also time to pay more attention to protecting our precious environment, thus the 'Green'."*

*Dennis believes that the people of the state urgently want a change of direction, and that the state could set an example for a similar change of direction by other states, as well as at the federal level, and help end the malaise that is gripping our country.*

*He will measure the response to this announcement before he makes a final decision. If enough of the state's business leaders show encouragement, and there also is strong public support, he intends to run.*

*For ten years Dennis served the state in the U.S. House of Representative. He was a steadfast moderate-conservative and strong environmentalist, before deciding not to run again two years ago. As a moderate-conservative he has fought for private enterprise, less federal government, more states' rights, lower taxation, less regulation, and a strong military. As an environmentalist he understands that environmental protection is good business, creates more rather than fewer jobs, and ethically is the right way to go. In a state so generously endowed with scenery and natural resources and so dependent upon all that tourism generates, we can't afford not to protect our environment. He also firmly believes ours is a capitalist society that relies on individual initiative, and not a welfare state.*

*He now is a practicing attorney in Bellingham, the city of his birth. He and his wife, Marge, have two children now in high school.*

At the group's next weekly lunch, after the meal is served and most have finished eating, I stand and, with the media release in hand, say, "You've all read Dave's release, as he revised it after receiving our suggestions. Are there any other changes?"

When none are offered, I turn to Dave and ask, "How do you plan to get the widest possible distribution?"

"I'll see that it's sent to all the state's media outlets, including press, radio, and TV. I'll also make sure that it gets national media and Webb exposure. And I should be able get all this done within the week."

"Sounds good. If it's apparent that there *is* strong business and citizen support, we'll pitch in and do everything possible to get Bob elected."

Dave's efforts produce widespread coverage and interest. It's front page copy in all the state's newspapers and other media outlets, and is widely reported and commented upon nationally on radio, television, and the Webb, and even makes the The Wall Street Journal, The Washington Post, The New York Times, and USA Today.

Reaction within the state is slow in coming. None of the major business leaders make a statement. When asked to comment, most merely say it's too early, or they need more time. Bob delays naming a campaign manager.

His announcement spurs two others to declare their candidacy, both Democrats. One is the state's attorney general, the other a liberal state senator from Seattle. The incumbent Governor, also a Democrat, reaffirms that she doesn't plan to seek reelection.

Seattle traditionally is 80 percent liberal, while the

rest of the state is about evenly divided between conservatives, liberals, and independents. In recent years, the Governor and both Senators have been Democrats, while most House members west of the Cascades are Democrats, and those east are Republicans. In close elections, the Seattle vote usually determines the outcome for statewide candidates in favor of Democrats.

But the next election promises to be a new ballgame because of the electorate's general disaffection with most politicians and almost everything political. A candidate with a fresh face and vibrant message should be able to win by swaying enough voters away from the traditional voting patterns. Once the general populace and the business leaders see that, they should rally in support of that candidate.

Bob will be an attractive candidate because of his relative youth and wholesome character and appearance, and because he is good at meeting and interacting with the media and public. He's also very intelligent and has a proven record as a successful and popular former congressman.

Before long he's being invited to appear on television, to meet with newspaper editorial boards, and to speak at chambers of commerce meetings and other gatherings who want to hear his message.

It's soon apparent that the prospect of Bob running has begun resonating among the electorate. When Bob learns that many of the big players are about to endorse him, he decides to formally declare his candidacy. An experienced campaign manager is enlisted, contributions start flowing to a newly created 'Dennis for Governor' campaign fund, and his candidacy is off and running.

Most of what Bob is achieving owes to his own personality, reputation, and efforts. Our group remains in the background, at least publicly, while still meeting regularly with him to offer advice and help. As President of a state funded university, I keep a low profile, but that doesn't stop me from pitching in.

Interestingly, the idea of a candidate talking up the Green Conservative philosophy begins being more a plus than a minus. The *green*, as expected, raises hackles, but Bob convincingly sells the idea that being green in Washington with all its natural wonders and reliance on tourism makes sense. He stresses that not only is protecting the environment good for business because it leads to more rather than fewer jobs, but it's ethically correct.

As our group had sensed, the state is ripe for change, even a sharp about-face, and it's looking as though Bob's approach will be a winner.

# Chapter Twenty-Six

**B**ob telephones that he needs to sound me out on a number of *thorny* matters having to do with his candidacy, and asks to meet.

Over lunch at the Faculty Club, Bob leads off. "Regularly now, as you know, I'm meeting with newspaper editorial boards, the media, and various groups and key individuals to lay out and explain my platform. In these meetings I'm having to contend with a much broader range of questions than those dealing with my plans for the state. The questions involve the nation, and even the world. It's almost as if I were seeking to be President, rather than Governor.

"Because of our close association all these years and our many discussions and activities together in Washington DC and here, I know that you keep abreast of all that's going on in the nation and world, as well as in the Northwest. So I respect your judgment and thoughts on the sort of questions I'm being asked."

Bob and I have been friends since I was a graduate student working on my MS degree. He's a few years older and more politically motivated, but with similar interests, beliefs, and love of the Northwest. We've often turned to each other for counsel and advice.

"I have my own ideas on how best to respond," Bob says, "but I'd like to hear yours. What I'll do is pose the questions to you, much as they're being asked of me, and then listen to what you have to say. It may help. Okay?"

"I'll do what I can, Bob. What's the first question?"

"One of the toughest questions I'm being asked is how can the US compete successfully with China, when its form of government enables quick and decisive problem solving, while ours is so lumbering and slow?"

"It won't be easy," I answer. "In the short run, because China's rulers can order things done and get quick results, they have the advantage. But in the long run, that advantage fades. Look what they're doing to their environment, and the disruptions they're causing their people. They have horrible pollution, and hundreds of millions are being displaced. Sooner or later those things are going to catch up to them. Millions will die of pollution-caused diseases, and millions more are likely to revolt.

"I believe that if we continue with the ideals that have served us so well, we'll prevail. But, no doubt, the competition is going to be very tough. And don't forget India. It's proving to be an almost equally tough competitor. What may determine the outcome is whether we're able to get our own house in order. While not predicting the outcome, I still feel safer being an American than the citizen of any other country."

"Picking up on your point of *getting our own house in order*, Pete, how is the mess in Washington DC ever going to be corrected, with the two parties at loggerheads and the Congress out of sync with the rest of the country?"

"The way I see it, for far too many years those with a liberal bent, both Democrats and Republicans, have been calling the shots, with the result that the country has eroded from being the vigorous capitalistic free-market society it once was, until it's now verging on becoming a welfare state, much as most of Europe already is. The reason the two parties are at loggerheads and the Congress out of sync, is that the *True Conservatives*, both those who are Democrats, and there a few, and those who are Republicans, finally are refusing to allow the country to continue down the road to socialism. They've dug in their heels! If the True Conservatives prevail, there's hope for the country. If they don't, then the country inevitably is going to end up like Europe. Somehow, some way, I believe a majority of the citizenry is going to see the light and rally around what the country's founders envisioned and what True Conservatives stand for."

"Another question I'm frequently asked, Pete, how is the country ever going to dig itself out of the $15 trillion hole it's dug itself into, when instead of balancing the budget, we continue racking up trillion dollar annual deficits, with no end in sight?"

"Unless and until we get back to where the federal government consistently is spending less than it's taking in, we won't dig ourselves out. Just as states and private citizens must live within their means, the federal government must as well. As a beginning, we've got to pull back from most of our overseas military commitments. As you know, as well as our deployments in Iraq and Afghanistan, the US now has 30,000 troops in South Korea, 40,000 in Japan, and 50,000 in Germany. Did you know, we even have 10,000 in Italy?

"Then, we've got to scale back our military establishment from a force designed to *police the world*, to one that while being fully capable of defending US borders and vital interests, won't be doing for all those other countries what they should be doing for themselves. And our military must be streamlined and modernized. Rather than relying on foot soldiers and tanks, it must be geared more to quick-response Special

Forces and Seal Teams and smart bombs and drones.

"Our space program must be wound down. It's a $17 billion per year *extravagance* with few really tangible benefits, other than satellites and telescopes. In addition,   tax loopholes must be closed,   most agricultural subsidies ended,   entitlement programs---Social Security, Medicare, and Medicaid---tightened, and Obamacare, which is nothing but socialized medicine, terminated.

"We must eliminate unreasonable regulations that hamper and constrict business, while at the same time carefully crafting regulations that prevent a repeat of what happened on Wall Street and in the housing sector that caused the Great Recession."

"Another question, Pete, how can the country ever become energy-independent when, because of its huge size and complexity, it unavoidably is dependent on the massive use of autos, trucks, trains, and planes to transport people and goods, and many of our own oil wells either are dry or soon to be?"

"There is no way the country can change its dependency on autos, trucks, trains, and planes, but it is possible to require more fuel efficient transportation, and to convert to other kinds of energy such as natural gas, electricity, hydrogen, and even atomic energy."

"That, then, raises the question of what the Arabs will do if and when we stop buying their oil."

"They're bound to do everything possible to prolong our dependency because of the consequences to them if we stop importing or cut way back. No doubt, they have huge cash reserves and for years have been diversifying and investing in other commercial ventures, which should help. But in the long run, because of the *foibles* of their religions and systems of government, and the way they are failing to equip and train their populace to be self-reliant and able to compete, it's going to be very difficult for them. The present unrest we're seeing over there is nothing to what it's almost sure to become."

"What about the *radical* Muslims and the terrorism they're inflicting? And, when if ever do you see the war-on-terror ending?"

"It's terrible that the *radicals*, while demeaning their own lives, have no compunction about disrupting other societies and sacrificing the innocent lives of anyone who stands in their way. Yet, that's what they're taught from childhood, and is what's behind their campaign of terror.

"The amount of blood and treasure we're sacrificing to fight the consequences of their evil intentions and actions are almost unfathomable. As well as all that Iraq and Afghanistan is costing, think of the trillions we're having to spend in making our airports and seaports safe and protecting our public places. Trillions we instead should be using to repair our deteriorating infrastructure and educate our children.

"Yet, I see no alternative. It's essential that we continue to protect ourselves as long as these *bad guys* are out there, even if it means committing additional trillions, with no end in sight.

"What's additionally alarming is that because the world's political, economic, social, and environmental pressures are steadily increasing, those committing terror, because they're the ones who are most affected by the increasing pressures, are likely to ramp up their terrorist activities, since that's all they understand. I don't see any solution, only a problem getting worse."

"What can we do about the almost two million Muslims already in the country, most of whom, it seems, are Muslims first and citizens second?"

"The best course is for us to go out of our way to *befriend* them and invite them into our society, hoping by so doing to *instill* in them a wish to be as good citizens as they are good Muslims. From all I read and hear, unlike the radicals, most Muslims have a peaceful intent. It's important, however, that we avoid happening here what's already happening in France, England, Sweden, and other European nations, where Muslims have immigrated in such numbers and are reproducing so rapidly that it's only a matter of time until they're in the majority.

"How are we going to cope with illegal immigration?"

"As you know, here in Washington, Mexican illegals harvest much if not most of our agricultural production and have for many years. Without their help, our harvests won't happen. So our farmers depend on them. The same is true in many other states. We must find a way to *legally* allow them into the country to harvest our crops, but to be accounted for so that after they stop working they *leave*. Any with aspirations to remain and become citizens, must take their place in line as everyone else".

"What do we do about the ten million illegals already residing in the country, many of whom have been here for years, with children born here who automatically are citizens?"

"That's a tough one, Bob. If they've established residences, are paying taxes, have children who already are citizens, and are employed, upstanding, solvent, and responsible, they're already de facto citizens. I don't see any alternative at some point to granting them full citizenship, but on a case-by-case basis. However, as to children born here to illegals automatically being citizens, that must end."

"Thanks, Pete, right now those are all my questions, recognizing that later I may have others. I appreciate your insight. All you've said makes sense and essentially echoes my own thinking. It's comforting to know that our ideas are so close. The country sure is facing difficult times. Many of its problems appear almost insurmountable."

"Yes, Bob, for way too many years the country's been run by well-intentioned but ineffective politicians, including a series of Presidents and Congresses without the wisdom or courage to face difficult challenges and find workable solutions. That's the reason for most of our problems."

"In one sense that's true, Pete. However, based on my experience as a former congressman, I believe another reason today's politicians are so ineffective is that they're hamstrung by a government whose *mechanism* over time has become overwhelmed and bogged-down with bureaucratic excesses and red-tape. If future leaders are to have much chance of succeeding, this mechanism needs somehow to be overhauled to streamline and make it more efficient and effective. The challenge will be doing it in ways that doesn't compromise the Constitution and Bill of Rights.

"That's an interesting idea, Bob. It makes sense. Maybe that's the reason for some of the dumb things that have happened and are happening back there. Why for instance have the floodgates been opened to such a massive flow of *legal* immigrants, many of whom it seems have little to offer in the way of skills or talent? Formerly, only well qualified people were permitted to immigrate.

"Why also haven't ways been devised to control *illegal* immigration? Granted, foreign labor's essential if our farm produce is going to be harvested, but it long since should have been *managed*.

"It may explain as well the present *impasse* in which almost nothing is being done back there, when there's so much that needs doing."

"Yes, Pete, and picking up on your point of the country being overrun with both legal and illegal immigrants, many lacking the abilities to get and hold jobs. As you know, many of them now rely on welfare and government handouts. So, who are they going to vote for? The answer of course is that they'll vote for whomever guarantees that the government *largesse* keeps coming, namely the liberals. This may well doom any chance the country has of returning to its conservative roots and of avoiding socialism.

"Still, Pete, don't despair. It's been a trait of every generation to say that things formerly were better, and the future is doomed. Yet, the future usually turns out to be brighter than ever. I hope that happens now."

"I hope so, too, but at least we need to be honest about these problems. Unless we square up to them, they'll never get solved. My advice in responding to all the questions you're being asked, Bob, is to simply say what you know in your heart is right and what you sincerely believe. Let the chips fall where they may. If people perceive that you're honest and forthright, they'll get behind you. The trouble with too many of today's politicians is that they would rather play it safe, to be politically correct, than tell it like it is.

"On a more personal note, I'm finding that one of the more frustrating aspects of *my* existence today is all the effort it's now taking me to escape the pressures of modern life. I formerly could drive a relatively few miles and have a stretch of river or a corner of wilderness to myself. No longer."

"All too true. Well, thanks Pete. Glad we've had a chance to mull over these very difficult questions."

Our time at lunch was a mite longer than usual, but I believe it was time well spent. Bob obviously wants to understand and be able to help cope with the horrendous problems that need to be faced.

# Chapter Twenty-Seven

Two months after Bob formally announces his candidacy for Governor, and after unending meetings with citizen groups, CEOs, editorial boards, environmentalists, and others to explain his approach and answer questions, major endorsements and contributions are being received. The big players are coming on board.

Not only are the state's corporate leaders buying onto the idea that they can make a huge difference in job creation by bringing jobs back and stimulating and assisting small business start-ups, but they actually are doing it. Hundreds of new jobs that wouldn't otherwise be available come on the market. They admit its costing them bottom-line dollars, but proclaim it's the patriotic thing to do and they're glad to accept the sacrifice.

From this show of support, it's evident that the business community and public-at-large are accepting the twin concepts of being *green* as well *conservative*. Even secular Seattle, always green, begrudgingly acquiesces in some respects. At long last they realize that if the needed changes are to happen, there must be some bend.

Thus, it's looking ever more likely that Bob is

going to be the next Governor. Neither of the other candidates is evoking much interest or enthusiasm, and it appears they'll soon be history.

The mushrooming success of Bob's efforts within the state galvanizes national media attention and major politicians and political parties. The Green Conservative plank that's attracting such widespread interest and support within the state also has created a stir nationally. There's even talk that Bob should forget about being Governor and instead try for the Presidency.

The Republican Party, never green, begins accepting the idea of being more environmental friendly, and even the inevitability of the new moniker, Green Conservative, at least within the state.

Pressure builds nation-wide on corporate leaders to emulate the strategies in Washington of bringing jobs back home and encouraging and assisting new small start-up companies.

The potential these strategies have of turning the country's faltering economy around is being recognized, and public confidence as well as the in-the-dumps stock market are responding.

Bob's campaign is now in full swing with big-time professionals in charge and he appears headed for a landslide, so our little group stands aside.

Leah and I sneak away for a week's fishing in Alaska, and she *arrows* an elk in the side canyon. More protein than we need, but Einar and Bruce and their growing families welcome the delicious steaks and roasts, as do Leah's mom and dad. There's even enough for friends.

Sluicing continues to be a relaxing way of spending a few hours, and because the price of gold is so high, even the few nuggets we collect makes the activity pay. Several times interlopers are reminded they're trespassing. Tom and Sally Strike tell us they're having the same problem along their claim.

Byron Hicks, now Dr. Hicks, is a popular assistant professor at the University. Yes, thanks to Leah, he's married to Jane, another young teacher.

Joyce and Dave Bennett are contentedly ensconced in Bellingham, she still as Dean of the University's Environmental Department, he as a syndicated newspaper columnist and published novelist.

Bob and Marge, our long-time close friends, are destined for the Governor's mansion in Olympia, and who knows what else.

My first inkling that trouble is brewing, is a call from Bob Dennis telling me he's just met with a reporter from National Exposer who's preparing an article about an affair Bob is accused he had with a former female staffer, some eight years earlier. According to the reporter, the former staffer came to the magazine and claimed that she and the congressman had engaged in a dalliance. She even provides details, including motel receipts.

Over lunch, Bob tells me, "I fired her as soon as she made sexual advances during one of my campaigns. She and I and other staffers were occupying separate rooms at the same motel. After being fired, she tried blackmailing me into giving her $25,000, or she said she would go public. I merely ignored her, and she never follow up, until now!"

I ask him if he reported it to the police. He says no.

"Then it comes down to your word, against hers?"

"I suppose so. In talking with the reporter, I of course denied the accusation and told my account of what really happened. But, as you know, that magazine makes a living sensationalizing issues like this. And because I'm receiving so much publicity, here as well as nationally, it looks like they may run with it."

"Who do you think put the woman up to it? I doubt she acted on her own. Someone had to have made it worthwhile and told her what to do."

"I asked the reporter and he said she voluntarily came to them. He admitted however that the magazine has agreed to pay her $50,000, *if* they go ahead with the story."

"Is Marge aware of any of this?"

"Yes, I've told her about the Exposer reporter, and in fact told her about the woman's effort to blackmail me at the time it happened, so she's known from the beginning."

"I'm still very curious about who's doing the *orchestrating*, Bob. I'd bet that some person or group opposed to your being elected Governor, and alarmed at all the attention you're getting nationally, has decided to torpedo you. Do you happen to know or suspect who it might be, or do you have a way of finding out?"

"I'm sure you're right, Pete. No, I don't know, but I'll put out feelers."

The next day a reporter from a Seattle newspaper comes to my office. "We *anonymously* received the tape of a long conversation you and Bob Dennis recently had that includes a number of controversial statements. We're considering doing an article. We had the conversation typed and I brought a copy. Would you care to see it and comment?"

I read through it, and as far as I remember it's a

verbatim of our conversation. Considering how best to respond, I answer, "I'll neither confirm nor deny anything. Any private conversation between Bob Dennis and me is privileged information and no one's business but ours."

"Okay, if that's all you're willing to say." And the reporter leaves.

Obviously, someone had covertly recorded our conversation and then delivered it to the newspaper. Obvious, also, an attempt is being made to disparage me in the same way an attempt is being made to disparage Bob, and the two must be linked. Because our friendship and long working relationship is well known, the culprit figures that embarrassing me will further embarrass Bob.

As soon as the reporter leaves, I call Bob and tell him what happened. I also ask if he's found out anything about who's behind his problem. He says he's still awaiting word.

A day later, Bob calls. "I've learned from my contacts back there that it's a group that fears Green Conservatism and my becoming Governor, and possibly even President. The group is funded by James Boros and they've vowed to do a hatchet job on me and anyone closely associated with me. Of course, with Boros, they have unlimited money and the kind of people who know how to dig up dirt on anyone."

Bob and I immediately meet with the masterminds behind his campaign and it's decided to beat the Boros crowd at their own game by going public with all we know about their efforts. Dave Bennett quickly prepares and disseminates a nationwide media release that exposes the treachery.

The hue and cry from NBC, the New York Times, and other leftist TV networks and newspapers, including the Seattle newspaper, is predictable, but only lends credence and tends to verify and substantiate what Dave included in his media release. Neither the National Exposer nor the Seattle newspaper follows up by publishing the hinted articles, and the attempt dies.

In the end, Bob becomes even more a national figure than he was before, and the flap only serves to enhance his election prospects.

# Chapter Twenty-Eight

Then, *TRAGEDY*!!! Bob Dennis, his campaign manager, and several staffers are killed when their plane crashes while trying to land at Yakima.

*Devastated*, all that his close friends are able to do is hang together and try to survive their profound grief. Not since my parents were killed when their auto was struck by a logging truck almost forty years ago, am I so stricken. Mainly, it's the loss of such a cherished friend, but also the apparent end of bright new prospects for the state and country.

Bob's campaign cornerstones, new small businesses and thousands of new jobs, already are bearing fruit, but without his energizing leadership, the harvest is uncertain, to say the least.

Two weeks after the calamitous event, Tom Strike calls and asks me to reserve the Faculty Club for our little group, and a few others. "It's time," he says, "that we begin picking up the pieces."

Noon finds Tom, Joyce and Dave Bennett, and Leah and me, seated and somberly studying our menus. To my surprise, we soon are joined by Bill Ewing, my former Dean at the University of Washington, Phyllis Redman, now president of a large university in eastern

Washington, the CEOs of Amazon, Starbucks, and Microsoft, and a Boeing vice-president.

Because Tom arranged the meeting, I wait for him to lead off, which, after we all order, he stands and does.

"Friends, thank you for being here today. As several of you suggested, I arranged this meeting in hopes that a way can be found to overcome our recent tragic loss and salvage what Bob Dennis would soon have achieved. It's a tall order, but we know the public now is counting on his plans for creating new businesses and jobs being realized, and we can't let them down. Most of what Bob set in motion is in place, but unless someone is able step in and carry Bob's ambitions forward, they may not endure. We need the right person to step up and carry on.

"I've already spoken with each of you about this and I know your ideas. We all agree that Pete, here, is *that* person. I haven't said anything either to Pete or Leah, so this no doubt comes as a bit of a surprise, but I hope that after thinking about it, he'll accept. Knowing Pete and Leah as well as I do, whatever the decision is will be made jointly."

Phyllis Redman, and then each of the others, stand and resolutely agree the Bob's promise must not be lost, and Pete's the right choice.

After everyone speaks, it's my turn, and for once words don't come easy. Rising, I pause to collect my thoughts, and then, haltingly, "Folks, this is unexpected, and I'm uncertain how to respond. Understandably, my feelings are mixed. I'm truly heartbroken because of our tragic loss; I'm humble because of what you're asking me to do; and I'm apprehensive because I'm not at all sure I'm up to the task of mounting a successful campaign and then, assuming I get elected, being an effective Governor. Bob was the perfect candidate. He fulfilled all those criteria. What a profound loss his death means.

"Right now, I have no idea what my answer will be. It certainly calls for some serious introspection and thought. As Tom mentioned, Leah and I need a little time. I promise to let you know what's decided within a few days."

Tom again stands and, thanking everyone for coming, dismisses the meeting.

Before leaving, Tom pulls Leah and me aside. "I didn't ask your thoughts ahead of time or even hint as to the meeting's purpose, because I was afraid you would reject the idea before giving yourself a chance to consider it."

Tom's right, I probably would have said no. Now

that there's time for us to think the idea through, I'm not sure what we'll decide.

Back home and following dinner that evening, Leah and I repose ourselves and begin weighing how to respond.

"It's vital that someone with the same beliefs as Bob takes his place so his plans don't flounder, but is it in me to do it?   I have some political experience from having worked closely with Bob in the state and in Washington DC, and as a Fish and Wildlife Commissioner and a university president, but I'm not nearly the politician Bob was."

"That may be, Pete, but it's clear from the meeting today that some very important people think you're up to the task."

"What about my religious beliefs, or lack thereof? Isn't that issue bound to surface, and once it does and the electorate learns I'm an *atheist*, won't that automatically doom my chances?"

"It well could.   We need to gauge how important an issue that is.   How can we find out?"

I pick up the phone and call Dave Bennett, explain the problem, and ask his help.   He knows a few who may have answers and says he'll see what they say.   The next day he calls back.

"Pete, I talked with some folks in the know who I respect, and it's their firm conviction that an atheist has almost no chance of being elected to a major political office in the state or country. They tell me that while there undoubtedly are some atheists in major political offices, right now there's only one who has declared himself. He's a member of the House of Representatives from San Francisco. He gets away with it by being from such a secular city. Actually, if it were alone up to Seattle, which is about as secular as San Francisco, you possibly could be elected, but elsewhere in the state, no."

"So, where does that leave us, Dave? Isn't it certain that sooner or later I'd be asked my views, or somehow people would find out?"

"Probably, but who else is there that has what it takes to fill in for Bob? The same group needs to meet again. Maybe they can figure out a way to resolve the problem? I'll call Tom and explain the dilemma and suggest that he arrange another meeting, okay?"

Several days later the same individuals have again gathered for lunch at the Faculty Club. Tom reviews the problem, and then opens it up for discussion. There is general agreement that an atheist has almost no chance of being elected as Governor, or to any other important post in the country. Most think it's unfortunate, but right now and for the indefinite future, it's a fact of life.

With time slipping by, no one offering anything tangible, and most getting restless, I decide to stand and tell them what I have  privately come to believe is the best solution.

"Folks, unless we're willing to risk letting this golden opportunity to turn things around in the state and even in the country slip out of our grasp, it's essential that we find a viable replacement for Bob. If she would agree to run, Phyllis Redman, here, would be an excellent candidate.  She's been a resident of the state for over fifteen years,  president of two of its major universities,  is well known, respected, admired, and widely  liked within the state and elsewhere in the country, and has the breadth of knowledge and experience a candidate and a Governor needs.  She also holds our same views about the need for change, and endorses the Green Conservative plank.  I firmly believe she could step in and fill the void." Then I sit down.

Joyce Bennett rises next and tells how she had been one of Phyllis's faculty members and how much she and others on the faculty admire and respect her and that the idea of her running for Governor is a natural.

It's evident that my comments and Joyce's endorsement echo others' sentiments. Several speak out, including the CEOs of Microsoft and Starbucks, saying they have the same feelings and strongly urge that Phyllis accept.

When Tom asks if the feeling is unanimous, everyone except Phyllis lifts a hand.

Tom then turns to Phyllis and invites her thoughts.

"I'm humbled that you would think of me, and honored to be asked. Just as with Pete several days ago, something as important as this calls for careful thought. I'll let you know within a few days."

As everyone is leaving, Phyllis motions me aside and with a friendly though faintly *wry* smile, whispers, "Darn you, Pete, for being an atheist."

Three days later Phyllis gets word to everyone that, although reluctant because of all her ongoing commitments, she agrees to run. "What's at stake is too vital to the state and country."

She soon names a campaign manager and the campaign for Governor is again back in high gear with many of the same prospects as when Bob was the candidate.

# *Epilogue*

Word of my religious views somehow has gotten around, and even though I'm not holding an elective office, results in a surprising amount of angst among some of the more pious elements in the state. There's talk that university presidents never should be atheists because of the bad example it sets for students and other young people. There are pro and con editorials and letters-to-the-editor and the issue becomes front page news.

While I decline numerous invitations to appear publicly to address the issue, I do release a simple statement that declares my belief:

*In response to questions about my views as an atheist, it is my carefully considered belief that certain yet not fully understood laws of physics and nature, rather than a God, a Heavenly Personage, always have been and always will be deciding the 'course of events' in our world and in the universe. I believe that once those immutable laws in all their complexity are fully understood, such perplexing unresolved questions as when time began, where space ends, how the spark of life came about, and, yes, even the destiny of man, finally will be answered.*

I would have preferred that my personal views hadn't surfaced in this manner, that I hadn't become a sort of *crucible*, but I'm not unhappy that the subject is receiving so much attention. Every time atheism becomes a matter of public discourse, the nation moves one step closer to accepting that people have as much right not to believe in God, as to believe in God. And that because someone is an atheist shouldn't disqualify that person from public office. In balance, atheists are no less worthy of being accorded leadership opportunities than are theists.

The University's Board of Regents meet with me and the subject is carefully considered. Predictably, probing questions about my point of view are raised. One of the regents, a distinguished church leader, asks a question that gets to the heart of the matter.

"What are your views about Jesus and do you reject his teachings?"

I reply, "Folks, because I'm an atheist, it goes without saying that I don't believe that Jesus was immaculately conceived, or that his teachings were divinely inspired. However, I do believe that Jesus lived, and that he was a great man, possibly the greatest, and a profoundly inspiring teacher. And I do affirm his views about morality, decency, goodness, and righteousness.

Upright men and women everywhere, atheists and theists alike, instinctively know that those views make sense and are right."

After a rather lengthy, interesting, and at times intense  discussion, in which the gist of my view  that atheists are just as capable and just as  inclined as theists to be upright citizens are hesitantly agreed with, most of the regents  vote to retain me as  University President. The Governor concurs.

In time, interest in the matter subsides, but not before it had excited a surprising amount of widespread controversy throughout the state, country, and even world.

Now that it's finally settled that I won't be running for Governor, or Representative, or any other major political office any time soon, or at least until the rights of atheists are generally accepted, it's possible for me to settle in and continue being as good a university president as I know how to be.  From my point of view, a not unhappy resolution of events.

*Finis*

# *Acknowledgments*

Few books are solo efforts, and this one is no exception. Barbara Y. Brown gave generously of her time and expertise with advice on style and content, as did Bob Martin. Special thanks to John Sager for sagacious ideas and editing. Blessings on son Clark who's always there when needed with timely advice and help. Blessings also on daughters Tanni and Shannon for encouragement and ideas. Finally, thanks to Google for being only a click away.

Cover image, courtesy Bob White.

## *About the Author*

Stan Young resides in the Pacific Northwest (Clyde Hill, WA), and has for the last 40 years. He was born, grew up, and attended college in Utah, twice served in the military, and retired from the Department of the Interior after 36 years. While with the Interior's Bureau of Outdoor Recreation and National Park Service, he helped among other things to get the Wild and Scenic Rivers and National Trails systems up and running. As well as being a life-long environmentalist, he also is an outdoorsman and, particularly, a steelhead fly fisher. His other book is "Twenty-One Years Fly Fishing for Steelhead," also published on Amazon.